Touch That Which We Cannot Possess

Jorge Armenteros

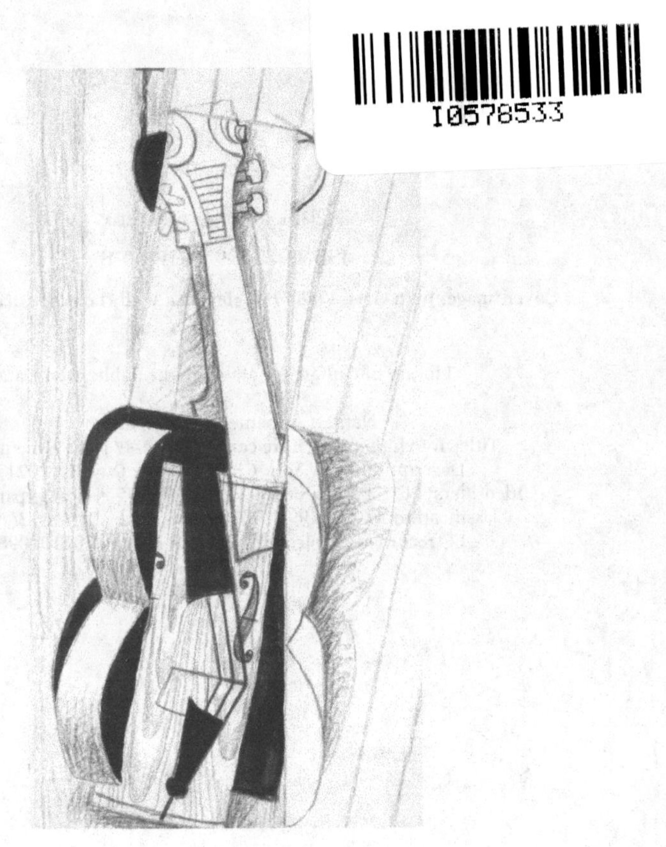

SPUYTEN DUYVIL

New York City

© 2021 Jorge Armenteros

ISBN 978-1-952419-50-8

Cover image: Juan Gris, *Violin Hanging on a Wall (Le violon accroché)*, 1913

Library of Congress Cataloging-in-Publication Data

Names: Armenteros, Jorge, author.
Title: Touch that which we cannot possess / Jorge Armenteros.
Description: New York City : Spuyten Duyvil, [2021] |
Identifiers: LCCN 2021000989 | ISBN 9781952419508 (paperback)
Classification: LCC PS3601.R5723 T68 2021 | DDC 813/.6--dc23
LC record available at https://lccn.loc.gov/2021000989

TOUCH THAT WHICH WE CANNOT POSSESS

PRELUDE

Naked, in the white, fully carved and scraped, my wood radiating a nubile hue, I await the first bath. My brother lies next to me, equally naked and expectant. I have not sung a single note. I am not fully clothed yet. My time is soon to come.

The master hovers over us, and the sound of stirred liquids floats in the hermetic air. I smell chimney soot, spring water, the urine of a child, alcohol, beeswax, oil; all coming together in this concoction bound to penetrate into our wooden fibers. At this point, my consciousness is shallow; I have yet to grow fully. Nevertheless, I know I embody another consciousness, older and larger—the consciousness of the sung and unsung instruments. Music is our core, our lifeline; and that is eternal.

The hands of the master begin to apply the first layer of varnish on my brother. The brush, bathed in the lustrous substance, licks my brother's back, his belly and inside his bouts. I observe as he becomes the prince he is bound to be—a full-blooded Venetian. But the master does not finish bathing my brother. He stops in the middle of the process. A weakness overtakes him, and he begins to shiver like a cane in the wind. He kneels on the ground and continues shivering and moaning in dialect. Without finishing the varnish ritual, the master leaves the workshop mumbling some words about God and the punishment of humanity. We are left as incomplete, half-formed instruments behind the black curtain of the workshop.

He has been absent for a few days, our master. I wonder if he forgot about us. The apprentices are also gone. Inside the workshop, nothing moves, only the hours; so, becoming our complete selves stagnates in a strange limbo. When morning comes again, our master returns to the workshop. He looks different, saddened as if death paid him a visit. While he prepares to finish applying the varnish on my brother, I notice an anomalous swelling and several black scabs on his neck. His lips are black, and so are his fingertips. Regardless of what assails him, he continues to work on my brother, layering a golden light on him with significant effort—this, a slow and painful rhythm that takes forever to come to an end. But when I regard my fully dressed brother, I marvel at his beauty.

The master seems intent on continuing to work and grabs my body with his blackened fingers. He dips the brush in the miraculous concoction, and when he is about to lap it on me, he starts to shiver again and drops the brush on the ground. He holds me tight, wanting to save me, wanting to save himself. But the strength drains out of his body and he loosens his grip on me. I fall to the ground, and like timber, he collapses on top of me—my body cracks.

Under the weight of his body, I begin to suffocate. I try to inhale through my f-holes, but the pain in my ribs becomes more and more intense. I bear the agony and wait for the master to roll away from me. But he remains immobile while his black fingers and lips become even blacker. I try to listen for his breath, but I hear nothing. I feel as if the mound on top of me becomes heavier, warmer, like black tar. Just when I was about to debut as a Venetian prince, I find myself buried under the weight of a black death.

The black cloth separating the workshop from the outside world does not move. Neither does the air inside the workshop. Unfinished, fractured, and suffocating, I cannot move. Slowly, I start to lose all sensations. My material body comes apart, and my consciousness begins to dissipate. I hope other hands will find my remains and recreate me as a wooden box. I hope music will find me.

*****

I abhor darkness. A torch on the wall emits a golden tone. And under the low ceilings, the tones bend over and fall, touching the ground and bouncing back to meet the ceiling again. A beautiful circle. Light is eternal; I believe it. But the corners of the room remain in darkness, and so do the long corridors that extend beyond the reach of the torch. What makes me cry is the sweating walls. They ooze and drip continuously, day and night. The particles of moisture impregnating the air land on my body and find their way between my wooden fibers. They make their bed inside my soft flesh, between my hard ridges. My voice changes then. Pushed over by the unwelcome company of moisture, I become obtuse. It takes days next to a coal fire to regain my voice. They all know that water hurts me. But no matter where in this place I come to rest, the waters in the canal penetrate rock and mortar and inevitably make the walls sweat.

In this ambit I sing the songs of volatile masters who walk down narrow passages, fearing they will be killed any moment; not because they carry any money, but because their music reaches beyond, further than anything the lesser composers can fathom. Setting your foot ahead can get your foot clobbered. Horrible, completely horrible. When the town becomes dark, when the mist fragments already flickering lights, the image of what we see becomes a spectacle, twisted and damaged. Some of the best music wants to touch that moment. I can feel it. But to write that music is to go against the grain, to sing in disparate ways. The walk of the iconoclasts is bound to lead them into a dark and narrow passage, a passage without exit.

Waiting in this small room in the company of three other instruments, bathed in darkness, I am surprised by the arrival of the composer in the company of a few players. He arrives with papers under his arm and the smell of fear, having crossed the town diagonally and ventured over begging arms. He lays the papers on top of the table and steps back to allow everyone to see. His eyes stay focused on the eyes of the players, reading their reactions. There, there is the music I yearn to embody. But the second violinist says he cannot play it, and the cellist says the same. The composer shows them a few other sheets. I managed to get a glimpse of a glorious passage for the first violin that makes me shiver. They all look at it and hesitate. The cello player says this will be a marvel, that they should make this happen. But nobody speaks for me, because at this moment no hands are set to play me. An orphan I am.

A sudden and precipitate exodus. Everything dissolves in a unison of emptiness. And darkness roars. Where there were people before, now there is nobody. People are now gone, but the music sheets are left behind on the table. I wonder if we are meant to sing that music. But if time takes its toll, the oozing waters will destroy the papers. What would then happen to the iconoclasts? I cannot tell. But what can I really do? Without the hands of the capable, I am nothing. This is when I wish I could… I wish I could. I rest in place waiting for a player to arrive. I simply hold my breath and maintain a certain air pressure inside my body. I hum a low hum.

*****

A man, a young man with no pretense, a young man dressed in rags, comes into the dark room and lifts me up as if I were his toy. He carries his own bow, a little longer than usual, and without hesitation, he starts to play Monteverdi. Nothing new, I know this music well. After exercising his music muscles, he lays me down and looks at the papers on the table. He seems intrigued. He takes a few minutes to read one page before turning to the next. While reading, his right hand moves up and down as if drawing the music in the air. He makes sounds with his mouth. He closes his eyes. I know he is drinking in the music and letting it traverse his body. The written notes and his silent movements intertwine to produce a visual interpretation of the music. He then removes his hat and sits at the table to continue reading the music. And once he repeats the opening bars in his head several times, he extends his arms and grabs me once more.

This time he grabs me with determination and purpose. I feel his grip, firm, visionary. He positions his left elbow west of my scroll, and at once, he plays everything. Not everything, but everything. He gives me the impetus I require to sing the most difficult passages with ease. He also shines in the adagio where the encounter between bow and strings begs for tenderness. And at the end of one hour, the young man shows a skill level superior to most other suitors. Why is he here? I do not know… but he is.

His hands move quickly, arranging the sheets and tucking

them inside his torn vest. He grabs me and runs towards the corridor where darkness awaits us both. Without a torch, he is lost. We are both lost. But he must know the way. He walks through the shadows for some time until we arrive at a much larger room lit with multiple torches reflecting their light on multiple mirrors. A few people are gathered around a woman who plays a green pianoforte in the center of the room. The mirrors on the walls repeat this image over and over until the pianoforte looks like a small toy. They stop playing the music at once and turn around to stare at us. In turn, I look at them as they look at us. And they grow in number, and I see myself in the mirrors over and over again, naked many times.

My ragged kidnapper jumps among the image planes dodging eyes and hands, ignoring the voice of the pianoforte, moving from the shadows into the torch-lit spaces. He glides, he appears in the corner of every mirror just to exit out by the opposite corner. And, within an instant, we are no longer exposed to the eyes of the pianoforte crowd. We go past the large room to find ourselves deep into another corridor where the shadows again dominate. He is moving me now, across space, across light, not across time, maybe across classes, or maybe across music. Where he is taking me, I cannot tell.

At the end of a long journey, after crossing multiple bridges over still waters, after escaping the menacing shadows of gargoyles and violent parapets, after getting drenched by the fine mist of heavenly waters ejected from the silver sky, after gliding inside the dark long hull of a quivering gondola; we arrive at the wet steps of a palace at the end of the canal. I feel like a sunken corpse, every fiber of my body entrapped by water molecules. I want to cough, but the wetness floods my throat. I am drowning.

Once inside the palace, he lays me down next to a wide fireplace vomiting heat and ashes before disappearing into the adjacent room. The radiant redness soothes me, and I allow myself to rest, my body fibers absorbing the intense vibration of the hot air. I hear him talking to other people in the distance. Many voices. They sound excited, or the pitch of their voices climbs in a way that sounds excited to me. I hear no other instruments, only human voices. And even though I lie alone, I have no fear. I accept the moment and my condition.

The voices die down abruptly. Maybe a prescribed silence, maybe a tacit agreement among them. Perhaps they try to listen to me. But I remain still and quiet, listening to the slapping of dirty water against the steps of the palace. A disquieting rhythm that is, the water hitting the stones hard, wanting to come inside. The fire speaks calmly, no drama in the flames, just the surrender of wooden flesh. I wait for other sounds to enter the room. Nothing. And all I hear is the melody of impending doom.

Still suffocated, I feel my belly swelling while my ribs desperately grab on to the seams. I feel bloated. The expansion stretches my neural chords making the bridge dig down on me. And I feel an uncomfortable pull from my scroll all the way down to my end button. I want to scream, but no sound comes out of me. And the pressure increases, and the fire is too slow, and the water molecules grow like cancer, and my A string screeches as it finally bursts, sending a sharp neural pain deep into my core… so deep. I am coming apart.

They enter the room and gather around me. My kidnapper loosens all my pegs, releasing the tension. I can breathe a little better now. He lays me down on the floor closer to the fire.

—This violin is garbage. Look at the bare wood.

—No, no, it has a wonderful sound.

—No way to tell now.

—I'll fix it. I'll give it a good coat of varnish.

—And what about the music?

—They match perfectly.

—I don't believe it. Too hard to play, plus this thing is all broken.

—I'll fix it. Then you'll hear.

—But what about the music?

—I told you, it's wonderful.

—Are you sure Giambattista wrote it?

—Yes, but it's even better than what you've heard before.

—Why so?

—It's wet.

—Wet?

—Yes… deep, oceanic, blue-green, still, and tempestuous.

—This violin is wet.

—I'll bring it back to life.

—Who's the maker?

—I'm not sure. Maybe Hieronimo Venier, but he's dead now.

—Bring it back, the poor bastard.

*****

Being wet is already a problem, but experiencing loneliness and a sense of abandonment bows me down. Half-deformed as I am, I can still hum Giambattista's new composition. He composed something extraordinary, and this ragged man knows it well. When he played me, he knew he was touching heaven. And he knew how to touch me, how to release my honest voice. I sang like a heavenly creature, and I like to sing that way. I know I can do that with the right score and the right hands. But in the darkness of that room, in the absence of an audience, the miracle will go unnoticed. Nobody will ever hear those notes again. They will dissipate in the air and ascend to the edge of the universe where nobody listens. That is art, a series of unnoticed miracles.

And if I were to consider all the notes heard in this world, many would sound just as heavenly. Besides the arranged music, the one in pentagrams played by expert hands, there is naïve music played by the hands of the untrained on the top of mountains and inside deep caves. There is the music of birds and elephants. There is the music of fish underwater. There is the music of falling leaves. And there is the music of the world spinning and the winds whirling. Just as heavenly, all of them. So why do we need instruments to create new sounds when the world already creates its own music. Maybe the creative spirit cannot resist the urge to imitate what surrounds it. Or maybe the creative spirit wants to play in the field of the gods.

Perhaps the nature of creativity is not vertical but horizontal. Perhaps there are no hierarchies, prescribed orders, or canonical convictions. The tree makes music as beautiful as the snake with its sinusoidal rhythm that sounds as mesmerizing as the storm ripping apart the earth with the cadence of its waves and the pizzicato of raindrops landing on the back of slaves who moan a song as ancient as all the hurt in the world. We are all playing in the field of the gods, creating when the gods are not looking.

*****

11

My flesh has a better color now—nothing like dry air and a good distance from the canal. Only the small lower angle of my C-bout harbors a dark fungus. It will disappear if light gets to me in the next few days. I need light, like I need dry air, like I need handsome hands to play me. I wonder if my voice will still be there, just like before. But why wonder? In the end, I am the same instrument I was, not much to speak of, but absolutely myself.

The ragged young man walks around me as if I were a diseased instrument. Maybe fearing a sort of contamination, he looks at me from a safe distance avoiding any accidental contact. The black fungus… maybe. But I feel nothing. Not a tingle or an itch. This is not the plague of his father or any other pest he may imagine. I am moving from wet to dry, nothing more. But regardless of what I think, he stays at a safe distance, forcing me to wait for welcoming hands to deliver me into the realm of the now.

He brings a chair into the room. He steps on it and reaches all the way up to a small window close to the ceiling. He struggles but manages to open the window allowing the sunlight to penetrate the room for the first time. The glorious rays make a diagonal impression, drawing a yellow rectangle on the floor, but missing my body. That is where I need to be, inside that box of radiant light. He must know how I feel for he takes the chair and places it inside the rectangle of light. And with utmost care, he takes me by the scroll and places me on top of the chair where the sunlight is quick to wrap itself around me. I want to thank him, I want to hum for him, but my body does not vibrate. Where have the butterflies gone?

With the passing of the hours and the movement of the sun, the lightbox changes its shape. It becomes longer and narrower. It also starts to move away from me, creating a sharp line that separates light from shadows. The line cuts through my body, slicing thin sections that fall one by one into the shadows. I watch the butchery until the shadows swallow my body completely. After a few hours of nothing but darkness, the moon peeks through the window and splashes its light all over my body. It also assumes a rectangular shape but carries no heat. In its whiteness, the moonlight touches my body, and I think of cold hands, wet hands, or the tongue of a salamander. The black fungus seems to relish the moonlight for it throws its little tentacles up in the air.

The cycle repeats itself, like clockwork, the sun and the moonlight alternating, the heat and the cold taking turns. My ribs shrink and expand, but as the cycles turn, the confines of my body seem to tighten. There may be less of me, or maybe I have become denser. After the seventh cycle, the young man comes back into the room and stands in front of me. He takes a rag to my black spots and wipes away the fungus, dry now, maybe dead. He picks me up and knocks on my back with his knuckles. I respond with a hollow sound, and for a moment, I vibrate on C. He turns me around and knocks on my belly. I vibrate on A sharp.

The young man sets me on the chair and leaves the room. I wonder where he is going. I wonder what he wants. He has brought me out of darker places before. And he has played me. With the help of Giambattista's music, he has played me superbly. I know he has to return with a plan, or at least with a yearning. I try to listen for other people, other instruments. Nothing. I contract my wooden fibers and keep a clenched silence and try to listen hard. But I hear nothing at all. I do not hear water slapping against rock, and that soothes me. But no voices…

Deeper into the eighth cycle, when I expect the moonlight to appear once more, the young man steps into the room carrying a bow and a little metal tool shaped like a bird's beak. He will dig into my innards, I fear. I remain calm and supple and breathe a shallow breath. He brings my body close to his face and inserts the metal tool through one of my f-holes. I stop breathing. He searches inside my body until he finds my sound-post. He pushes it around; he fondles it. Then he digs in with the bow making me sing a scale. He goes back in and taps my sound-post again. I feel the tiny movements and the itch shooting from my belly to my back. He plays a few scales, turns my four pegs, and plays a few more scales. When he is satisfied, he takes the metal tool out of my f-hole and lays me to rest on the chair.

He opens his vest and takes out several sheets of music and begins to read them. His face glows. At once, he takes hold of me and prepares to play me. He lays the sheet music on the chair where the sunlight shines on them. I recognize the slant of the notes, the singular punctuation. Giambattista? Yes… Giambattista. But unknown to me, faster, bolder. And he launches into the piece like a jaguar, to the neck, all at once. Playing for an imaginary audience, he projects my voice beyond the walls of the room, to the last rows of an imaginary theater. My voice sings each note with a dry clarity I had not expected, lighter, and more resonant than before. Bravo for the hands that play me! Bravo for my survival! Bravo for this new piece by Giambattista!

*****

The ninth cycle ushers a pleasant surprise. The young man appears with a pot and a brush. I recognize the smell at once: divine varnish. If I were to remain raw, in the white, I would definitively lose my tone over the years to come. To attain a distinctive timbre, I need to be bathed in that lustrous substance. I wonder what his formula is, what ingredients he blends, and in what proportions? Perhaps he has knowledge that comes from the old masters in Brescia, those from the last century.

With care, he begins to apply the warm translucent varnish to every corner of my body. He seems concerned only with transparency, with preserving the wood underneath. I relax and breathe long deep breaths allowing my bare wood fibers to open up and receive the balsam. I watch as my body begins to glow under the soft lights filtering through the window, and I marvel at the magnificent golden yellow tone.

The varnish, however, imparts a certain heaviness to my body. I could not sing a single note in this condition. And the young man seems to understand the way I feel for he does not try to play me. Instead, he allows me to rest for several cycles. I have lost track of how many. But I know he expects me to sing at my best, soon, fully dressed and glowing.

*****

Three other instruments surround me, Venetians all of them, and the tall ceiling looking abysmal. I could fall into it. From my position, I could. But I decide to bear all my weight down into the dry ground and project my voice up. I am willing to let my voice fly up and away, into the vast spaces trapped by the tall ceiling. If I let my voice hover above the heads of the audience, the sound will create caverns of its own. And those caverns will have ceilings, maybe tall ceilings. At this point, I just want to sing my best. I want to fill this room with my roar.

Men and women in stiff garments gather around in close proximity to each other. The smell of one body mixing with the smell of another. They recognize each other by their smell, like animals, which is exactly what they are. So different from my existence. My body does not secrete fluids. I do not stink. Unless my wood was to rot; a horrible consideration. If I were to smell as putrid as the old man who sits next to me this very moment, I would have my body thrown into the canal. With a hacking laugh, this man transacts a conversation with the young man who will play me. The putrid man says virtually nothing, and my raptor and savior seems to recognize the baseness of the exchange. Finally, all the bodies sit down in stiff chairs and silence their voices. The air does not carry any more superfluous utterances, but it carries the stench of the conglomerate up to the tall ceilings above.

The young man produces the sheet music he has been hoarding. The other three musicians take a serious look and seem perplexed. They exchange a few words, point at various places in the pentagram, and eventually bring their hands down next to their instruments. The audience, clustered together as if there was no room in the vastness of this palace, looks at the four musicians in anticipation.

—We're gathered here at the Palazzo Aggio for an exceptional occasion. The composition you're about to hear is a gift. Giambattista hasn't shared this with anybody else. We hope you'll enjoy the music.

What they are about to hear is a miracle, even if they have no capacity to recognize it. My body and the body of the other three Venetians will vibrate in unison, also in disagreement. We will interpret what Giambattista conceived, and this interpretation will escape our bodies. We will fail to retain the miracle inside ourselves; it will twirl around the stinking bodies of the audience, ascend to the voluminous ceilings, and eventually breathe itself away. The air in this room will not retain a memory of these vibrations. The audience will recognize they experienced something special, but they will not understand they barely touched immortality.

We launch ourselves into the piece with no clear sense of the magnitude of the moment. We make our way through the newness, tinged by recognizable twitches, but an unprecedented experience nonetheless. Yes, this is Giambattista, and his signature style is all over the piece. But as we advance in this unrehearsed adventure, we enter landscapes we never saw as instruments. We skid across ice under the relentless fall of icy rain; we encounter sleeping goats and barking dogs, drunken dancers turn and turn around us while insects buzz viciously. And instead of a uniform front, where the four of us would sing alternating roles, I become the singular instrument to project my voice over the basso continuo of the other three. Of the four, I become the one. I have never taken a position as prominent as this, and the young man seems enthralled with the experience. He enjoys the response of the audience, and the more they express admiration, the more they salivate, the louder he plays me. My ribs want to burst; my belly wants to give birth to this new creation. Are we deaf? Why has music not existed like this before?

The music resonates inside the room for some time after

we finish playing. And when the audience descends from the ecstasy, an uncomfortable sense of dampness entraps their feet. The lagoon, accompanied by the pestilence, has been slipping under the door. The source of all evil, this water is certain to usher in plague-bringing venomous snakes. People start pushing each other as they rush to the door, hoping to escape from this flooding room. The high windows offer no escape. But when they open the door, more of the lagoon enters the room. The *palades* are not holding. In desperation, the young man leaves me on top of the table and makes a mad rush to the door, rising his arms in horror. I come to rest next to the other three Venetians who, like myself, lie recumbent and abandoned.

The lagoon, black as black, black as the death that took so many hands, rises inside the room. The still surface of the water gradually ascends, aiming to reach the ceiling and obliterate us all. The lagoon faces no resistance; it merely occupies the room at will. Through the window, the night fails to shine. At this time, I fear I will drown. On my back, I resign to my condition as an instrument for the hands of others, with a voice of my own, but with no capacity to move across the earth. My voice travels fast and far while my wooden body is planted. And the hours pass, this I know, not because the stars tell me, for they are black themselves, but because I continue to play Giambattista's music and keep the rhythm of time.

At dawn, when a feeble light makes its way through the window, I find myself dry. The three Venetians remain next to me on top of the table, their bodies intact. The lagoon has claimed most of the room and its docile back is only marred by the swimming rodents who desperately try to climb on top of the dry table. On a corner of the room, the sheet music floats feebly, and the black ink becomes one with the black waters.

THE AWAKENING

As the waters recede, they leave a film of scum attached to the stucco. What used to be a delectable ochre, now wears a greenish maroon mask. But with no living hands within earshot, I am left alone in silent contemplation of this color, a reminder that nothing ever remains. With time, the scum turns even darker and assumes a powdery texture while still clinging stubbornly to the stucco. The three of my mates rest next to me, emitting no sound whatsoever. I try to listen for the faintest sign of vibratory life, but I hear nothing. And nothing is what I have heard for a long, long time.

Twice per day, the water swells outside, and I can hear it slapping against the stone walls. It wants to come in again, the water, but it fails to clear the windowsills. I am happy not to see that again like I am happy not to see the rodents swimming in desperation. I have come to detest when light becomes scant, and the air turns cold. My body feels like shrinking then. But the worst is when the air turns warm and humid. This tends to happen when there is ample light. During those days, or months, my body feels bloated, and my seams want to break open. Somehow, I stay intact, but I fear what would happen if one day I were to burst apart violently. What a horrible thought!

I try to remember some of my favorite passages to play in my mind. Sometimes I recall entire concerts. Mostly, I remember the touch of the hands that played me, and the music associated with those hands. When the hands that played me were vulgar or maladroit, what remains of that music is a caterwaul. When I am not remembering past performances, I focus on the music at hand. The lapping of the water that is. This undulating and crystalline crash of fluid molecules creates such complex harmonies that they are capable of inspiring a legion of symphonies. And I would not be surprised if Bach and Giambattista were secret wave devotees.

Inside this room, surrounded by this implacable decay, I am forced to wonder whatever happened to all that music I have sung. Does music have a destiny of its own? Once played, are the melodic vibrations doomed to die a quiet death or do they continue to travel up in the sky into a sort of aural eternity? Maybe all the music of all times has ascended high above the earth and coalesced to form a sonic dome. This dome, growing and expanding by the addition of every melody played by all the people and all the musical instruments over times immemorial. What a wonderful dome that would be.

*****

A strange commotion of people accompanied by a stranger commotion of voices enters the room. I have not heard a voice in so long. How long I cannot tell. And the light. How bright now, after so much darkness. And so yellow, an unreal sun it seems. Uncertain of the meaning of this assault, I remain supine and immobile. Their hands poke me and push me aside to the edge of the table. They place the bodies of the other comatose instruments next to me. Why this now? Why the lights? This is not a stage, and these are not musicians. Where has the music gone?

—Why so dark? Turn those lights on.

—They'll see us.

—No, they won't. Nobody is looking.

—Is that better?

—Much better, but turn it down just a little.

—There?

—Yeah.

—How about this one?

—No, look at the crack next to the end button.

—That can be fixed.

—Yeah, maybe.

—This one's worse, a completely broken neck.

—Too bad.

—How about this cello? It looks pretty good.

—Seventeenth century.

—For sure?

—Absolutely.

—What else? What else?

—There must be a viola somewhere.

The room seems familiar, but different at the same time. I think I slept here. But not on my back, standing maybe? This room, so small and so full of everything. I hear them rummaging through drawers, lamps, books. They seem to be exhuming everything. Around me, all things turned upside down and the dust flying.

—Here it is!

—Not bad this viola.

—Yeah, in much better shape than the violins.

—How much are these worth?

—I don't know, but someone in this town will know.

—When are they coming?

—Don't worry, we have time.

Time. They have time. Do I have time? And what sort of time are they referring to? What sort of time is this? I could wait here for something to happen, for time to reveal itself. I could also scream and hope for the playing hands to come for me. But where are those hands that played me? Are they gone? Is this the black death again? This must be a different order, or maybe a different dream. I remain still and try to identify the sounds that filter from the outside. No bells; I do not hear them. Giambattista, where are you?

This is a room I recognize, but these two men are unfamiliar to me. And their way of handling me, the atrocity of their gestures, is something I have never felt before. They push me as if I were a piece of cheese. Brutes they are. And as I look at the violin next to me, as I come to fathom its broken neck, I wonder to what degree I am hurt myself. I feel a discomfort in my bottom, but that could be the result of standing for so long. Or perhaps I am broken, cracked, fractured around the end bottom.

This is bizarre. I am in this habitual place but surrounded by so much hurt. And to aggravate the situation, confused about time. If this were the Palazzo Aggio, the softest of hands would be lifting me. Instead, these rugged fingers poke my ribs. So, I look at every corner, I consider the height of the ceiling, I behold the frescos on the walls, I inhale the stale air, and I conclude that this *is* the Palazzo Aggio. Yes, but there is something disturbingly wrong.

The two men disappear for a while. I wonder if they will ever come back. But my wonderings are shattered by their sudden arrival; this time accompanied by a short man with glasses perched on the tip of his nose and a musty smell, the smell of someone who just descended from an attic. This short man lifts the prostrated violin next to me, and after careful examination, he lays it down. He then picks me up, takes a long look at my body, turns me around and upside down, runs his finger down my purfling, knocks on my back a few times, looks into my f-holes, and to my disgust, takes a needle and punctures the skin of my belly. I scream; I think I do, but everyone ignores my plight.

I hear voices galloping outside the room. Advancing, growing larger, the voices force the three men to hold their breaths and assume a concerned expression on their faces. In a mad rush, the cello, the viola, the moribund violin, and myself are thrown inside a chest, and its cover slammed shut. How dark, how dark.

—What's inside this room?

—Nothing of interest.

—Can you get all this shit out of here?

—Yeah.

—Smells bad.

—What do you expect?

—The larger rooms are perfect for the exhibition, but they want to use these smaller rooms as well.

—We'll take everything out. It's all garbage anyway.

—What's inside this chest?

—More garbage.

—Take it all out.

—What are they showing here?

—The *Venice Biennale*. Weird art. All sort of contemporary crap.

Then all the voices die out. Only the darkness remains. And time gets all confused once more. But at some point, hours or days later, I cannot tell, the chest with my stringed bedfellows is carried away from this room to another place that smells more like the face of a blonde woman.

Ever since I can remember. And for how long can I remember? For as long as that may be. I have never, never, been thrown around like this. And if the pain in my body is substantial, even more painful is the absence of music, for I have been moved around, in a daze, tangled with these crippled instruments I no longer recognize, enclosed inside dark spaces against my will. My will? And all along, with no sense of musicality, no notes or harmony, only silence.

Someone finally opens the chest, and light comes flooding in. This must be early in the morning for the light contains no red hues. The short man I saw before with the glasses on his nose, peers inside the chest. He pushes the other bodies to the side and pulls me up. When he lays me on a mahogany table, I take a good look at this very unusual room where I find myself: a low ceiling, many straight angles, and a chandelier with non-flickering lights. And on top of an adjacent table, the most peculiar silver frame, and in its center, moving images.

He aligns my body with the edge of the table. He pulls the other violin, the viola, and the cello out of the chest and lays them next to me. An army of defeated soldiers, bruised, fractured, and with no voice left. He then takes a little brush and proceeds to wipe our bodies, sweeping away dust and mold alike. Pushing his glasses back up his nose, he takes a long look at the four of us. And I feel defenseless, our damaged bodies exposed to the world, our wounds for all to see. Somehow, I believe this man takes pleasure in our misery. I truly believe so.

Then the sound of someone knocking at a door interrupts his inspection. A crowd of six or seven people come directly to our table and begin to touch our bodies. Their obscene hands have their way with me. I try to complain, I try to scream, but my voice is silent, and so are the voices of the fellow instruments next to me. We are inaudible.

I lose sense of time and place. A curtain falls. There is no applause. A curtain rises, and an intense light bathes my body, a liquid light, interrupted by the shadow of moving hands, or fishes. I stop feeling. And without a sense of touch I float, my body weightless, the crack on my bottom now painless, no stiffness in my neck. I try to conjure a melody, a simple passage, but the well of notes is empty, eviscerated. I try to listen for another music, the music of the viola, or the cello; but I hear nothing. Where has the music gone? And if there is no music, and if I cannot feel my body, do I exist? Do I?

The moment I regain a crystalized vision of the little man with the glasses, I realize I am resting alone on the mahogany table. The other instruments are no longer beside me. With a measuring tape in his hands, this man sizes my body. He measures the length of my fingerboard, the width of my bouts, the size of the f-holes. He measures everything. He writes it all down on a small black notebook that he puts away inside his vest pocket. He takes a few steps back and stares at me for a long time. I wonder why I am here alone. I wonder what he wants.

*****

The tall walls are covered with paintings that are not paintings. They do not portray people or landscapes. It looks like someone just dropped paint on those canvases and smeared them with their feet. Yes, their feet, because their hands could not be so clumsy. One of them is a large rect-angle with nothing but the color black. Maybe they have not finished it yet. And that image on the wall, a moving image, like the camera obscura but on its feet and moving contin-uously. I just wonder why nobody reacts to these paintings. The audience moves quietly around the room, seemingly ad-miring those grotesque blotches of color. They actually look at them as if they were looking at something.

In the corner of the room, next to this oversized fortepi-ano, a young woman holds me with studied tenderness. And without my permission, she begins to play me. Beethoven's Violin Sonata No.3. How lovely! The notes of the *Allegro con Spirito* emanate from the fortepiano and sound rather loud. I never heard anything like it. The tremendous size of the fortepiano may be the reason. So, I project a little louder and manage to create a beautiful sound. I proceed through the movements while watching the ebb and flow of the audience. They seem to enjoy the music, but nobody pays any special attention to us. The audience is seriously invested in looking at the strange paintings on the walls. At the end of the third movement, the young woman takes me down a hallway into another room where a gigantic mass of iron in the shape of a horse lies on the floor. Dead, I suppose. Here we are joined by another young woman with a cello. I think I recognize the cello, although I am not so sure. My young mistress starts to play me again, forming a most interesting duet with the cello. The music seems to ascend, so light it feels. I cannot distin-guish a clear melody. One phrase grows out of another in a refreshing organic way. They announced it as a piece from Maurice Ravel. I have never heard that name.

And from that room we move on to another room dominated by two windows adorned with latticework. My young mistress starts to play Bach's Partita for Violin Solo No. 2, and I feel more at home except for the strange looking candelabra hanging from the center of the room that seems to shine without burning anything. I take a peek through the window, and the water in the canal threatens me. I sing my best when there is no water in sight. Even knowing that water is nearby hinders my resonance. But water is ubiquitous. This city, surrounded by water, even threatened by water, is my crib, my sore lullaby.

My mistress moves on to the next partita with ease and delicacy. For such a young age, her touch is assertive. I like assertive hands, hands that play me with intent. The brutes I detest, with their heavy touch and lack of sophistication. I have been played by many of them. But their faces, their intense and empty faces, I cannot remember now. A man once said I sounded like a cherub. I do not remember who he was, nor when he said that. And I have a hard time imagining how a cherub is supposed to sound. Angelical, perhaps. Or maybe like a child, a screaming child. But the suggestion that I sound in some peculiar way has always intrigued me. Here, in this massive hall, I hope to sound eternal. Which raises the question of time and how we change over time. Is my voice the same as it has always been? If I were to project a G sharp on the D string, would it remain sharp forever, or would it lose tension with time and become a natural G, or even an F sharp? How do people treat sound over time? Would the melodies of the geniuses, Bach, for example, be always beloved? And considering how bodies deteriorate, would I be able to vibrate in the same way I vibrated for *La Tempesta di Mare* when I am older? Would I be there for Giambattista when Giambattista is no longer there?

From the large hall with the tall windows, we move to an open courtyard where a fountain spits water, and the winds are free to visit. More instruments come to join my mistress and I. Two violas, the cello I saw earlier plus a second one, and one very shiny violin that looks strange to me. The six of us gather around the fountain and the music of Boccherini fills the entire courtyard. And this is when I come to realize that something essentially wrong is happening with me. I feel like my singing voice is fresh, but the other instruments sound as if they are singing in a stilted ancient voice; as if they were remembering how to sing. I do not know what to make of this, so I continue to project my voice as best as I can. And the water droplets in the fountain seem to know what we want to say; they jump high in the air before diving into the communal body below, at the rhythm of an *allegro moderato.*

Water is life; it jumps and runs; it dribbles and splashes. But water is also death; it can lie on its back and rest recumbent, eternally still, until its very nature turns into vapid vapor and flies away. And I wonder if music is like water, in its life form as well as in its death form. Music can be life; I know that. Nothing livelier than a string quartet when unleashed. But can music be death as well? Not the music that pretends to imitate death, like a requiem, but music that invites the end of all things. When I sing the *Dies Irae* in any of its iterations, Bach or Verdi, am I courting death? Am I slashing the veins of those who play me? I only wonder. But if music is supposed to express all things human, fears, aspirations, and illusions, death has to be integral to the process. And I wonder if I have died before. Has my voice been silenced, extricated from my body? Have I existed as wood only? Not as a resonant box, but as the very dry substrate of my body? I wonder if I grew tall in the woods.

The courtyard, with people listening and instruments playing, feels as comfortable as any of my memories of the days before this day. Even when people look a little different, their clothes primarily, I sense their acceptance of music and their understanding of the progressions that will deliver them to a place they could not get on their own. And the courtyard provides the stage for this miracle. We sing, the other instruments and I, and we provide life, mostly life. And somehow, I feel a deep bond with the young hands that play me, the girl, maybe the woman, but clearly a bond exists with the sensitivity of her touch. And when I try to identify people and places, all I can identify is the mist rising from the fountain, water again, with its life and death motifs.

The tempo of the day changes very little. We continue singing and moving from the courtyard to the interior halls of the palazzo as people continue to admire the absurd paintings and each other, they gaze at each other, I can tell, while paying little importance to our music. And when dusk drops a hint of color over the canal, the crowds begin to vanish and the walls grow tall again making the palazzo more recognizable to me. The other instruments also vanish together with the hands that were playing them. My mistress, still holding me with her soft hands, retires into a small room where she sits down for the first time the entire day on a worn-out green divan. She moves slightly to one side of the divan and places me next to her. Out of a leather bag, she pulls out a small flask of what I think is cognac and takes a long, deep drink. I feel the warmth of her body; I also feel the coldness of her solitude. She takes another drink, not so long this time. She then picks me up and holds my body at eye level.

—Who are you?

What a devastating question. I wish I could give an accurate answer. I am music; I am wood, I am nothing unless played. I am a consciousness, maybe a mathematical equation. I could also be a simulacrum, the false representation of what I am supposed to be. Maybe I am old, or maybe I was born in that room with the bludgeoned bodies of my three quartet cousins.

—You sound like an angel from the past.

But how to describe my sound when I depend on hands, like her hands, to bow me, to press my fingerboard on the right spots, to breathe with me, vibrate with me, to project a common voice? I am, but I am not. I sound, but I sound not. And at this moment, the questions loom larger than the walls, and my answers are as empty of meaning as the paintings on the same walls.

When everything becomes quiet, when the halls reach absolute emptiness, my mistress places me into the case and starts walking away with me. Her determinate steps go over wood, stones, and gravel. She must be traversing narrow paths and crowded streets. At times I hear the water of the canal crashing against a seawall or the hull of a boat, and that makes me tremble. She keeps on walking for a while, less than an hour, I think, for no bells toll during her walk. And when she finally stops walking, she places my case over a hard surface. A voice I recognize approaches from afar. Then they open my case, and the little man with the glasses I had met before, hovers all over me again, the inquisitive little pest. He takes me out of the case and places me on a hard mahogany table. Am I about to be fondled again? I cannot take this.

—What do you think? Is it better than the other violin?

—Nothing special.

—How can you say that?

—I prefer the other violin. This one is dull.

My mistress picks me up from the table and turns away from the little man. As she brings me in front of her eyes again, I feel her hands beginning to tremble. She seems troubled, as if confronting a deep abyss in front of her. I realize she is lying.

—But they seem to come from the same maker, you know.

—Maybe, but this is a lesser violin.

—A lesser violin?

—Yes. Where's the other one?

—I sold it already.

—What a pity.

—How much would you pay for this violin?

—Nothing, really.

—Well, it's not that bad. Offer something.

—Not for this bastard.

—Fine, I'll find something else for you. Let me keep looking.

—I hope you will. Find something with a pedigree and a sound to go with it.

—I'll keep on looking. Take this one for now.

—The bastard?

—Yes, Kiara. Take it with you.

THE UNDERWORLD

Motion and darkness, motion, and darkness. Who knows how much time passed since I last saw a glimmer of light? This is not a familiar place, at least not familiar to me. But Kiara moves around with ease and a sense of belonging. This must be her home or at least a place where she behaves as herself. The walls in this room are particularly short as if the room has been beheaded. No blood, just dust, and a loud clanging noise coming from a metal spiral that irradiates heat, for there is no fireplace in this cold room.

I find myself next to another violin, not my brother, the one I lost in the Palazzo Aggio, but an ordinary looking one. Who am I to pass judgment on my own kind? Best to stay quiet until I learn more about this place. And I do. I just observe as Kiara sets a music stand next to the table where I rest with the other violin. She pulls some sheet music out of the top drawer of a dark desk and clips it to the stand. She then grabs this other violin and begins to play. I just listen—the mesmerizing notes of *The Art of Fugue* rain on me. And I am happy, transported, found again in this unknown place. Kiara plays with grace, modulating every note and making the violin sound infinite. I feel my ribs expanding, my back starting to vibrate, and my belly wanting. A low elemental note emanates from my body, a note not played, the very essence of who I am in the presence of greatness. I sing untouched, unbowed, immaculate.

Kiara lays the violin back on the table. It looks exhausted, this violin. But I sense a glowing and deep satisfaction coming from this instrument. Maybe it had the most satisfying orgasm of its life. And I lie here, hoping that Kiara will do unto me as she did unto it. But she goes away from the table, leaving me there, wanting. I hear her voice talking to another person whose voice I cannot hear. There is no answering voice, only silence. She speaks into a small rectangular box and laughs. The timbre of her laugh is supreme. And the sound of the other person is nowhere. When she finishes talking to that ghost, she picks me up from the table and dips her chin into my bout. She presses down on me, nothing between her skin and mine. I feel the weight of her face, the weight of her mind, a mind full of musical notes ready to be born.

Kiara bows me, unleashing a chase without an object, her notes fleeting without persecution; this a lonely fugue where her voice is not answered. Without counterpoint, Kiara's voice is my voice, the notes coming into this world through her, through me. An ageless communion. I feel I exist as a fugue in my mind alone. But, all of a sudden, she lays me to rest on the table and picks up the other violin once more. This violin, accelerating the rhythm, now answering my voice. The harmonic impulse mounts, with its tension, creating a dialogue between the other and myself. Kiara lets the other violin rest for a moment and takes me in her hands again. I project my voice with enough force to counter any emerging phrase from my doppelgänger. I grow. But she then substitutes me for the other one, who retorts. And then I sing, and then the other violin sings, and we continue chasing each other, the two of us, growing like crystals until we reach the divine or something akin to it.

At the end of the fugue, the other violin and I come to a point of agreement. We know each other's song, and we respect it. Together, we sound like each other, but each other sounds like itself. And the sense of otherness only exists when we yearn for Kiara's touch. When we try to usurp her talent, we become each other's other. But when we let her play us with abandonment, we both sound supreme. And with this thought in mind, I come to rest on the table, my doppelgänger next to me, and I breathe deeply.

The night begins. And from the table where I am resting, I see a window across the room that opens to a vastness. A field of twinkling lights spreads wide outside the window. The lights penetrate deep into the horizon, and some escalate the night, forming tall and mesmerizing vertical alignments. Sounds come in, many sounds. I hear trumpets and horns, loud screeches from deranged violins, and a massive chorus of passers-by, a river of them. The energy outside continues incessantly for hours until the night ends.

With the morning comes that uneasy sense of anxiety that burrows deep into my belly. Not knowing what the day will bring or what hands will play me is a devastating sensation. The anxiety has come to visit me every morning, at every place, for as long as I can remember. This is when I try to stay still, avoiding unwanted vibrations, relaxing my spine and loosening my neural cords. But the sudden eruption of a resurgent Kiara breaks the morning spell and ignites my awareness. She runs around the place gathering all sort of objects which she puts into a bag. She throws me into my case and shuts the cover with force. And just as quick, I find myself hanging from her shoulder while she takes me somewhere, somewhere.

I hear many steps and the voices of many people. We descend a long stairway. We keep descending but without the sound of steps as if floating on a magical carpet. When we come to a stop, Kiara places my case on the floor and opens the cover. The place in front of me looks like Dante's Inferno, a massive tunnel with a vaulted ceiling. And many people, hundreds, stand at the edge of the tunnel as if anticipating something. A sudden wind pushes from inside the tunnel, and within seconds, a hissing iron serpent makes its way and comes to rest in front of us. It opens its flank, and people exit and enter its belly. And just as swiftly as it appeared, it scurries deep into the tunnel and disappears at once. And nobody around me seems disturbed or marveled by this occurrence.

And in front of this continuous coming and going of people, Kiara picks me up from the case and starts playing me. She simply stands there, ignoring everyone, even the repeated visits from that iron serpent, while she makes me sing the beautiful Albinoni's Adagio. Over and over she plays the same excerpt to an ever-changing audience who only listens for a few bars before moving away in haste. Some people drop coins in my case and I do not understand why they do this. The disordered ambiance creates an uneasy feeling and my voice starts to quiver. Is this what they call a circus? An underground circus?

A man approaches Kiara and starts a conversation with her. She lays me in the case and continues to talk about music with the stranger. They seem to like what each other is saying, the bright expression on their faces tells me. But I have a hard time listening to their conversation because the noise in the tunnel is rather intense, especially when the iron serpent makes its entry, which it does this very moment. And, without notice, the hand of a thief shuts down the cover of my case, smashing me against the scattered coins. Then I feel a hard tug. The thief rushes into the belly of the iron serpent which disappears into the tunnel, hissing.

*****

People next to more people, hanging from metal tubes like monkeys, inside the belly of the snake that moves fast, stops, and then moves again. The snake braces the back portion of its body while pushing and extending the front portion. Then it drops its front and straightens and pulls its back, like throwing itself forward, a concertina, a beautiful motion. The large crowd remains silent; nobody talks, nobody looks at anybody. Then an immense person dressed in rags, and smelling as if part of him has died, leans closer to where I am held, between the legs of the thief who snatched me and begins to speak.

—What's your instrument?

—A violin.

—You play for real?

—Sort of.

—Sort of what?

—Play.

—Can I play it?

—I don't think so.

—Why? 'cause I'm fat?

—No, not that.

—Lemme play.

—Cut it out.

The large man gets up from his seat and stands in front of me. I fear his immensity. He begins to sway from one leg to another while hanging by one hand from the metal tubes. His shirt does not cover him completely; a significant amount of flesh spills over and hangs exposed. I see blotches of a crusted, yellowish substance covering some of his exposed skin and I remember the days when people melted in the streets of Venice, everyone keeping their distance, and a stench not different from the one he emanates.

—I hear the music and the voices in my head.

—Sure.

—They tell me to play it.

—Please, don't touch the violin.

—I wanna eat it.

—Step away from me.

—I wanna eat it.

The large man lets go of the metal tube, kneels on the floor, and looks at me with such intensity that I truly think he is about to bite my scroll off. At this time, the serpent comes to an abrupt stop making him fall on his back, his vast body pouring over the floor. People step aside; a little dog chirps.

—I'm gonna eat you.

—You fucking lunatic!

The thief jumps over the rolling immensity of the aggressor and rushes outside the belly of the serpent before its flanks seal up again. And the two of us join the river of people. The flow takes us up a set of stairs, around a few corners, until we emerge out in the world of light. I hear the bells marking the time of day in such a mechanical way that I wonder if they are real.

The gloomy expression on people's faces makes me believe a large sorrow has inflicted this town. We walk fast among the walkers and little changes from one street to the next. This must be a very sad place, or something very sad must have happened in this place. The fast pace makes my case bang against the thigh of the thief, an *agitato* rhythm that promises to break me apart. We carry on for several blocks, the thief and I, until we come to a sudden stop where I am placed on the ground, a wet ground and the acrid smell of decomposed food impregnates my case. I know not to move. I know to recoil to prevent touching whatever the impregnating substance may be. But before I begin to absorb anything fetid, the motion, the *agitato* rhythm, begins anew. I lose track of the distance traveled; I lose track of time. All I feel is the rhythmic banging and my mind falling into a trance. Here but not here, I am.

An array of voices gathers around me as I come to a shallow awareness in the middle of a large room devoid of any saving grace, for the walls lack paint and the chandelier right on top of me spits a pale light. Five or six people share a common cigarette, passing it from mouth to mouth, a strange form of smoking. One person pokes me in the belly and starts laughing. Another pulls hard on my strings. They all start laughing at once as if taunting me was the biggest joke ever. I was expecting one of them to lift me and play a few bars, but they seem content with looking at me as I lie inside my open case. The thief pushes the others apart and stares at me with those red-river eyes.

—A beauty, isn't it?

—Where from?

—Grand Central Station.

—Did you really?

—Gotta be quick.

—What the fuck, you can't play this.

—Says who?

—You bitch, you know music like I know shit.

—Watch me.

The thief pulls me out of the case and lays me on his left shoulder. He takes the bow, and without tensing the Mongol hair, starts scratching my strings with no sense of rhythm, clowning mechanically, pushing hard against my bridge. He carries on and on, jumping up and down and scratching my neck. He then stops and looks around, proud, as if he had finished a Paganini concerto. The others laugh, they laugh, and the idiocy falls out of their lips like molten teeth.

But what is a violin to do? Am I a servant? Am I a slave? The hands that play me come from different walks of life. Am I a link to their desolate deities, or perhaps a semi-god that sings celestial harmonies? Am I just an instrument, a mechanical device that produces sound? Or, more bluntly: Am I nothing? Nothing. Nothingness. These questions are real to me, but I doubt the thief has ever pondered them. And for that reason, I know I have to find a way to escape. I have to find myself a different setting. I have to leap into another place, maybe another time.

Now they share a pipe, short, and what they burn is not tobacco. That acrid smoke rises from the common pipe, and they all want to take it into their lungs. They take turns smoking this pipe. And the more they partake, the more they forget I exist. Alone, completely forgotten, I watch the revelers play games among themselves, making faces, pushing and pulling, kissing and biting each other. One of them yanks the pipe out of someone else's mouth. This unleashes a chain reaction. A fist lands on the territory of a face, a foot ventures deep into someone's belly, an earring gets pulled, tearing the delicate tip of an earlobe—blood of course—a body falls flat on the floor, the head following afterward and hitting the floor hard, an elbow finds a neck, and the sound of pain pierces the air; this, a horribly dissonant chord.

The thief tries to exert some level of control by hitting the others harder than they hit him. And he seems to succeed, for many bodies find themselves on the floor, looking at him in expectation. They want another chance to smoke the common pipe. And they get what they want. The pipe circulates, and most get another puff, except one of them who receives the hard edge of a boot against his jaw as opposed to the chance to draw smoke from the pipe. He squeals as he runs to the door and leaves the place screaming profanities. The rest of the revelers are happy to stay. This I know because their faces glow. I do not want to glow; I want to transmute, or at least, find myself elsewhere.

The thief seems to be an important figure among this crowd of imbeciles. He dominates them by means of that pipe. They look up to him, expecting, waiting to receive that most beloved smoke. He does not explain much; he takes action. And in a sweeping gesture, the thief buries me inside my case and pulls the whole contraption up. And watching his indentured servants with a cold eye, he walks away with me on tow, into the streets once again. We join the flow of people. The walking mass, rubbing their shoulders, elbows, and worn-out lives with each other. And as we move through the human cacophony, I perk my ear for the chance to hear a melody, any composed harmony that would elevate me beyond the baseness of the day. But all I hear is noise, the white blur of confusion, the sound of unreason.

At a fast pace we move through this city exuding an elemental sadness. Dull colors dominate because the sun barely reaches the sidewalks. The buildings grow tall with no regard for the scale of those walking between them. I have seen ugliness before, but nothing of this magnitude. A grand, magnificent horror this city seems to be. And after walking and turning, and turning and walking, we enter a shop containing row after row of violins hanging from pegs on the walls. This is not a museum, a mausoleum for my species it seems. The thief does not look at any of the instruments; he simply walks straight to a table in the back of the shop, drops my case flat, opens the cover, and exposes my belly.

The store owner, with a white beard and a cloudy eye, comes around to take a look at me. He lifts me out of the case and turns me around, his good eye inspecting every corner of my body. He brings his nose close to me and sniffs my bouts, my back, my f-holes. He then taps my belly with his knuckles while listening to the echo of my wood. He laughs loudly, and spit dribbles out of his mouth landing on me. He turns around and starts talking to the thief.

—Where did you get this piece of shit?

—What do you mean?

—Piece of shit. Where did you get it?

—It belonged to my grandfather.

—Well, your granddaddy wasn't a good player. Was he?

—How much do you give me?

—I give you shit for it.

—C'mon, give me something.

—Son, this is worth nothing.

—I heard a woman play it in the subway and it sounded great.

—You said it belonged to your granddaddy.

—It did.

—Yeah, yeah, yeah… I give you 50 dollars.

—No, 100 dollars.

—Listen, I'll give you 60 dollars and that's all I'm paying for this clunker.

The thief takes the cash, puts it in his pocket, and walks out the store without looking back. I have been sold before. I have been traded, always without my consent. But never before have I been disposed of as a piece of cheap meat.

*****

My condition, a wooden box that vibrates when played. Play me. And when their hands do, my ribs expand and my chest bursts. I sing. Sometimes I cry. But without the scratch of Mongolian hair on my neural cords and the poking of fingertips on my neck, my words would die in silence.

I hang on the wall, not at eye level, that is for the Cremonese. My row is lower and longer—more of us here. Several generations of dust particles weigh my shoulders down. And the only reason he picks me up, this young man, is because the store owner wants to get rid of me even at a loss, tired of me, I guess. Something I cannot understand, for the store owner, with his white beard and a cloudy eye, has never heard me sing. But this youngster seems inspired. He lays me on his left shoulder, holds me down with his beardless chin, and takes me from one scale to the next, all the way to seven sharps. Yes, he is young, but not a debutant. Then he rips through me with the opening lines of the Bruch Violin Concerto. He stops to regard my body and then plays the melody again. He smiles; he drinks my sound. He then does the unthinkable, bursts into an array of improvised notes. Jazz, I think they call this, which makes me reconsider the way I ought to sing. The little devil!

After the store owner hears him play, he quickly suggests another violin for the youngster to audition.

—For not much more money, given your skill.

—But this one's perfect for me. Who's the maker?

—Unmarked, perhaps German, but not Chinese. Now, this one over here *is* a fine instrument.

He pulls out a Cremonese from the top row and points at the label inside the body. He hands it to the young man who refuses to play a single note on the noble instrument.

—Don't be afraid; we have a loan program.

—No, I want this other one.

—Well, it's not even marked. You can do better.

—I'm not sure I can do any better.

—Why don't you bring both violins to your teacher and let him or her choose the best one?

—I don't have a teacher.

—You don't?

—No, I don't.

—Then take this lesser one and be happy. It's German, I think.

And like many times before, I do not see the exchange of money, which makes me feel a notch better than a prostitute. Clearly, I do not sing for money, but for the right touch. And the touch of this devil is an irreverent one, and I want more.

With his red hair and brazen attitude, I would follow him to the end of the world. I wonder what music they play in that world. Would they still play the dead ones, or would it be all improvisation, polyrhythms, and syncopation? The end of the world… who knows?

The little devil brings me down into the underworld where I once saw the iron serpent. And after traveling for a while in that dungeon, he brings me up into the upper world again. He starts walking fast and avoids talking to anybody.

We eventually arrive at an industrial building in what they call Bushwick. I feel like we have come to the end of a great civilization, for no other town known to me has pockets hoarding so much devastation. He drags me up the stairs to a room with dirty windows and a musty smell. He takes me out of the case and watches me. Never like this, nobody has ever watched me this way. And without hesitation, he digs in. My voice comes out twisted, bent, and tortuously juxtaposed. I emit a voluptuous sound in double stops, triple stops. I feel the immense pressure of his bow on my neural cords. And I reverberate in ways I never knew before; all to the absorbing silence of badly plastered walls, and the slanted eyes of a slumbering cat.

He talks to a few people on that little box and makes arrangements for the evening. I cannot tell what those people are saying, but he seems to command them. He mentions a bar called Korsakoff. And that foretells the psychosis, the confabulatory madness, and the amnesia that will follow a night of profane music. And under the pressure of one hour after the next, the night explodes—a signal of the madness to come. I think of madness when perhaps I should be thinking of new vibratory experiences. Even better, I should be thinking about hidden folds in my voice, folds untouched by menacing spiraling smoke particles.

Once we arrive at the location of the bar, we encounter a door losing its skin and marked with an exaggerated calligraphic "K." And beyond the door a stair leads us down into a small room where people seem too close to each other. Everyone we come across wants to greet him, and many look at me as they would look at a new mistress, with flagrant curiosity. There is a stage, maybe an altar, and he lays me there unaccompanied, while he goes to fetch his first drink. As I watch the human mass swallowing him, the sound of fractured voices drills holes into my body. A rancid miasma of smoke, sweat, alcohol, and the cacophony of other instruments hangs in the air.

A few people climb on top of the altar dragging their instruments. Some I do not recognize, like a pair of wooden cylinders with dried animal skin stretched tight over one end. We are cramped here, and I start to suffocate under the dimmed lights. Someone picks me up, a woman I do not recognize, and she starts to tantalize me, not playing me, just feeling my cords. I do not sing; I simply purr under the delectable touch. There is laughter amid the sound of loose notes on the altar, not a melody, notes as if fallen from the lips of a drunken god. Others start to follow, adding notes of their own with no apparent aim or tonal intention. There are silences too, short ones, some equivocal, merely hinted. And nobody in the tumultuous audience seems to realize that music is being born. There is only confusion or the prelude of amnesia. The little devil returns swirling a glass of something black, which he sets on a nearby table. He pulls me away from the delicate hands of the woman, and without much reverence, bows down on me. I sing an obtuse note, I breathe, and then I sing another. Am I sounding dark or luminous? I wish I knew.

Hands join the effort of other hands, and for a moment, all notes come to an arrest, a sudden death. All eyes on the altar gaze at each other netting a diabolical web. The old man with the saxophone gazes at the slender white woman with the clarinet, who in turn gazes at the black man with the cello, who looks down for a moment before lifting his gaze and darting at the mulatto with the wooden cylinder and skin contraption. A long pause. Even agony. And without any signal, my little devil begins to play my G string in a rhythm that makes me feel eternal. I expand, and every recess within me feels full, inundated by an organic sense of being as if I always existed in this mode, oceanic, my voice before mankind.

As the night rides, the conflagration of melodies becomes more intriguing. Different people step up to the altar to bleed their instruments, and the resulting composition defies my tonal preconception. There is order, but order of another kind: syncopated magic. And without formal hierarchy, the players occupy spaces as they see fit. They recede into the background, move forward, and step down from the altar; sometimes they sit on the floor or walk into the heaving thickness of the audience. This freedom intoxicates me as much as the alcohol and fumes intoxicate everyone in this dungeon. And the night rides on.

The little devil hands me back to the young woman that held me at the start of the night. The first thing I notice is the softness of her touch. I recognize that touch. She presses my neural cords with her fingers. And she slides the bow with a known angelical pressure. She seems to exist in a space of her own, separate from the tumultuous array of players that crowd the altar. I sing as if I have sung for her before. I speak to her. Kiara? Kiara? And from the way the little devil looks at her, I gather he yearns for her touch as much as I do.

I am breathing the strangest air. The lights die down. I lose track of time again. Is it Kiara who holds me now? Could these be her hands? Then a piercing silence breaks the spell. She steps down from the altar and finds my new red-haired owner deep in a conversation with another girl, both smoking, sharing a makeshift cigarette. She caresses my back before turning me over to him.

—This violin sounds great!

—Just got it.

—Temperamental… Don't you think?

—Why do you say so?

—I don't know. I feel it cuts through me, in a familiar form. It reminds me of Venice and the Biennale. Plus, it shifted on me on the third position.

—A wolf note?

—No, more like a lament.

No, not a lament. Ecstasy. Ecstasy from her reclaimed touch. The sound between common notes. My voice unencumbered. This is how I sound without sheet music, outside the confines of the pentagram, under the spell of her hands.

Kiara draws from the little cigarette, now shared by the three of them. No more words are exchanged. They seem content with listening to the bass marking a nocturnal rhythm, like the heartbeat of an insomniac horse. She then pulls a red case closer to her, and from the inside she pulls out another violin. And with the same ease as she held me before, she grabs this violin and returns to the altar. As she joins with the other instruments, I feel like a voyeur, watching her hands touch that other violin, watching the impetus of her gliding bow.

We remain at the Korsakoff until everyone has had enough. Enough music, enough alcohol, enough madness. And before the impending amnesia descends on us all, I take a long look at Kiara and her vulgar violin. They seem at ease, content even. They belong to those species that bond with each other, complementing, enhancing, mystifying themselves in front of the world, creating a union that feeds on itself, destined to last. And I feel like I want to land in her hands again and be held for a long time, making music, burying my innermost wood inside her spirit. Play me Kiara, play me again, and let us sing the unsung.

*****

I think we travel through time, or maybe we only travel through confused spaces. But at the end of a syncopated serpent ride and through a chaotic morning light, we arrive at the apartment with the dirty windows. The little devil, tired, lays me on a table occupying the center of the room and goes to his bed where he collapses, a tired hero and a wasted drunk. I rest on my open case and relax the tension in my ribs. I stay quiet, humming at a very low frequency, inaudible, simply savoring the melodic diaspora of the previous night. The improvised music played tricks on me, the little devil ripped through the core of my experience, and Kiara touched me again. What a delicious triplet!

Deep into the day, after the sun has already filtered through the dirty windows in oblique angles, the little devil tempests out of his room. He swirls, moving fast around the apartment and mumbling to himself. He goes into the kitchen, and I hear all sorts of noises, some high-pitched, a whistle, a bell. He comes around and sits at the table with a cup of coffee. And for a long time, he just looks at me. I lie there, exposed, naked, my body reflecting the muddy light. I hold his gaze while contemplating the red languor of his hair. His face shows a sinister peace, like the quiet bars of the Ninth

Symphony before the eruption of the choir. Something must be troubling him, or something must have become evident in this early afternoon. I cannot tell.

Holding the little box, he disappears into the bedroom to talk to people. I hear his words from afar, blurred, distressing the meaning of the conversation. The tempo of his voice is rushed, *andante*, maybe *vivace con brio*. And when he comes out of the bedroom, his eyes are not as contemplative as before. He picks me up and holds me tight between his chin and his shoulder. But this time he does not play me; he just keeps me there; close to his face but far away from music. And I know that what started yesterday is about to change—from my bat status, hanging at the lower level of the violin dealers shelf, to the hands of the little devil, to the irreverence of night music at the Korsakoff, towards something that I feel but cannot pronounce.

Just as I am about to abdicate to the chaotic side of fate, the doorbell rings. And without waiting for a response, Kiara bursts into the room with the imminence of people who want. She must have done this before, for the angle of her brow shows a splendid comfort. The little devil seems happy to dismantle the stiffness of the afternoon hours and lets Kiara into his room. They speak briefly, and I can hear them, and I think they know that. Maybe they want to make me aware of their doubts, or maybe they are just lovers, simple amateurs who fail at the task of safeguarding their secrets.

—For how long are you going?

—I don't know. Until I find work.

—That could be a long time.

—Yes, but I need to go.

—So, what do you want from me?

—I'm taking that violin.

—Wait, I just got it.

—I know, just the same.

—Why that violin?

—Something familiar. The voice, mainly the voice. Or a tortured memory from Venice.

—Yes, it's tortured.

—Perhaps, but it speaks to me. Or it has spoken to me before.

—Really? It's a cheap thing, you know.

—Yes, cheap, it doesn't matter.

Towards the unknown into the hands of Kiara. Could this be glory? Glory only if I could sing from the depth of my body. This is my nature, to pour music into a measure of time, to glide from one phrase to another, to fill the air with vibrations. But then there is her touch. Is anyone's touch essential to my nature as a violin? Is my voice independent of my wooden nature, independent of the hands that play me? I barely have an answer, but I welcome the labyrinth of my uncertainties.

THE
DISCOVERY

I was devastated when Kiara turned me over to this bitch Madeleine. Was it the money, or the chance to play in front of royalty? Just when I thought glory had come my way, just when her touch was entering my daily existence, I was exchanged one more time. Maybe Kiara needed to touch money more than she needed to touch me. Or perhaps she thought it would be a temporary arrangement. I need to understand Kiara's motivations for exchanging me. Regardless of any logical explanation, reality remains the same for me: the brute plays me while angelical Kiara watches. Yearning for her touch is corporeal—yearning for her desire is eternal.

What's worse is that Madeleine plays me as if I were her slave—ordering me around as if I had no say in the matter of tone. She thinks she creates music, with her left hand, with her bow. What she does not understand is that I vibrate at will; that I sing to impress or to undermine. Yes, my name and fortune are directly tied to her hands, but I am the one who generates the sound. Ultimately, I utter the voice people actually hear.

All of a sudden, I find myself under a crushing pressure that fractures my thin bridge. I immediately feel the loss of tension in my cords. I am mute now, hurt, and mute. Madeleine has probably done this on purpose, thinking that I refused to stay in tune. But not this time. She missed her notes of her own accord. When she walks out on the stage to beg for charity, to collect whatever applause the embarrassed audience will give her; she leaves me behind and hides me from the public. She needs to conceal the injury, the abuse.

Two glasses of champagne. That is all she needs to become erratic. One glass works well, but the second one takes her over the limit. Colder days are better; she does not drink as much then. But there is no fresh air to be had in this horrible summer, and the feeling of suffocation is real. The *Palais Princier* is as beautiful as it is scorching. Particularly when there is no sea breeze to bring relief to this overheated Monte Carlo. Kiara played a convincing second violin today earning her fraction of the applause. I wait backstage until they both return. Kiara takes me on her hands and seems bothered by my fractured bridge.

—Madeleine, what happened to the bridge?

—It broke. Bad quality, I guess.

—A *Despiau*?

—Yes, but still…

—It looks sad like this.

—Well, this violin lacks consistency. Some days I'm marveled, even mesmerized. Some days I want to kill it.

—You don't have to keep it. I can take it back.

—No, my dear, this is a fine violin. It plays well, and I need to impress at the *Opéra de Nice*. But it seems to have a mind of its own.

—The violin?

A mind of my own… Not only a mind of my own but a whole body and a concept of music as well. Madeleine plays notes as if doubting, hoping for the magic to happen by chance. She expects my body to perform superbly, precisely, unaltered by mood and circumstance. But I cannot help to feel bored sometimes, especially when I have to utter dead sounds of dead composers to insensible dead ears. There is no applause in the world that can make up for such deadness. There is something to be said about contemporary composers. I heard what jazz could do, and I am forever spoiled, corrupted.

If we are going to play at the *Opéra de Nice* tomorrow, someone will have to pay attention to my broken bridge. And with most people at the beach or down in Corsica, who would take care of my wounds? A rough woodworker? Who knows, but there is nothing I can do to change my fate at this point.

Madeleine straps my case around her shoulder and hops on her little red Aprila. She traverses narrow streets, goes up and down, making sharp turns, all the while the Aprila making an obscene amount of noise considering its size. When we arrive in Nice, the crowds get thicker. More mopeds and more people, and everyone wanting to cross the street right in front of us. She maneuvers around all these obstacles to arrive at rue Berlioz, a name that elevates my hopes for getting appropriate help.

Inside the luthier's shop hang the inner organs of my kind, decapitated bodies, spinal cords, loose pegs, skin naked and exposed. His hands, the most abused hands I have ever seen in a luthier, grab me tightly. Does this man toil in the fields when he is not cracking ribs? When he touches me, I try to tense my body, but all I manage to do is open up my belly even more. It hurts, and I try to cry as loud as I can. But no sound comes out of my body. I am muted, silenced without a gag.

When he starts to unwind my neural cords, I sense a kindness that disarms me. The brute is not a brute. In spite of having those horrific thick fingers, he manages to clean my wounds with care and softness. He tells Madeleine that I will be fine and that she should come for me tomorrow afternoon before the concert at the *Opéra de Nice*. Madeleine knows my capacity and expects I will perform for her. But inside, I know she despises me. She should despise her own failings instead.

The luthier works on me in the late afternoon which gives me the opportunity to watch him for a while. The most unusual tics become evident. Every five minutes or so, he seems compelled to pull down his left earlobe, sneeze, and shake his head. The entire routine takes less than a second. He is very fast. But when a client walks into the shop, he manages to keep his composure and suppresses all tics. The head shaking or the messing with his ears are acceptable, but sneezing over me is not. And the frequency of the tics increases the more he focuses on delicate tasks. When he is setting the new bridge, carefully positioning the wooden piece on the right spot, he goes through at least seven cycles of the tic routine. The spray emanating from his nose lands on me, and I feel mortified, soiled. But luckily, when he finishes the operation, he sets me aside before readjusting my cords. I breathe, I think I cry, and all I wish to do is jump in the sea and wash his excretions. The sea is nearby, but I doubt anyone would think of throwing me into its body. Eventually, he approaches me with a rag, a dirty thing, and wipes my body half-clean.

Later in the evening, while hanging like a bat on the wall, an imposing man walks through the door of the shop as if he owned the world. He brings with him an old case, and from its depths, he pulls out a sad looking violin with a deep crack radiating from one of the f-holes. He talks to the luthier, does not smile at all, and turns his gaze towards me.

—To whom does this violin belong?

—Madeleine. Do you know Madeleine?

—I don't think so. What's wrong with it?

—She broke the bridge.

—On purpose?

—I don't know.

—It looks like a Stainer.

—More like a mongrel.

—Is it tuned?

—No, but go ahead, tune it if you want.

The man turns my pegs until my voice resonates clearly. He borrows a bow from the luthier and proceeds to play the opening solo from Sibelius Violin Concerto in D minor. Welcoming the excitement, I demonstrate the balance and sound of my voice. I spill my guts. He keeps on playing more intricate passages, like Paganini's Caprice No. 24 in A minor. A master, no hesitation, perfect intonation, and with a focus that seems malicious. He dislodges me from his tight grip and proceeds to inspect every angle of my body. He regards my neck, my scroll, and he looks deep into my f-holes. I feel violated.

He sets me down on the table next to the wounded violin he brought along. I watch him, and his facial expression reveals a combination of sadness and excitement. I cannot tell. He starts to breathe hard and half-closes his eyes. Meanwhile, I just lie here, exposed, next to this moribund violin that makes me want to scream. I hold back my voice; in turn, the man is the one who screams.

—Phenomenal, what do we have here?

—Not a bad sound.

—What do you mean? This is excellent.

—Well… Its factory made.

—Are you sure?

—Madeleine said so. And there's no label.

—Labels lie. How old do you think it is?

—Can't tell how old it is. The one-piece back is excellent, look at the flame. But I don't know about the purfling.

—Italian? German?

—Sounds like both, don't you think?

The man picks me up again. He re-examines every angle of my body. This time he taps my back, my belly, and runs his fingers down my neck. He pucks one of his nostrils into my left f-hole and inhales deeply. He then retrieves his own bow from the case he brought along and launches with full gusto into the Lark Ascending. I flutter, I fly high, and the notes reverberate, like the wings of the delicate bird, into the contained air of the luthier's shop. I open up; I love the sound of my voice when he plays me.

—When is this Madeleine coming back?

—Tomorrow, she's playing at the *Opéra*.

—Tell her I want to meet her. I'll be at that concert tomorrow.

The man is very quick to finish his business at the shop, leaving the sad violin for needed repairs. Once he is gone, the luthier lays down the infirm on a dusty workbench in the back of the store. I get a premonition that the violin will die there, abandoned. How sad! The luthier comes around to take a closer look at my body. He takes a sharp metal tool and scrapes a minuscule flake of varnish from inside my right C-bout. He grasps the flake with a pair of needle-nose pliers and looks at it against the light filtering through the door. He then takes a measuring tape and begins to size my proportions. He writes the numbers down. And then he introduces a small mirror through one of my f-holes to look inside my gut, sickening. Once the luthier finishes with his examination, he puts me back in my case.

Why do they care so much to know where I come from? Why is it so important? I can sing. That is what really matters. Even when played by inept fingers, I can vibrate beautifully. I wonder if knowing my origins would make me sing differently? If I were from Cremona, would that make me sound better, more sublime? Or would they think I sound better *because* I came from Cremona? I may be a bastard child, the ignored creation of a master, or the product of a machine from China, or from Mittenwald at the turn of the century. I may be nothing more than the wooden box that holds my voice, a voice that always existed, before any of them dreamed of playing a violin, a voice that belongs to nobody, that flows errant looking for a space to fill. I could be a collection of random vibrations in the air, or I could be the incarnation of the minds of the masters, like Bach and Paganini, their audible dreams. Maybe I am nothing and I do not even exist. Maybe I am a voice in the forest that only noble beasts can hear.

*****

At the *Opéra*, the concert becomes what it has to—a questionable display of artistry. The exemption being Kiara who plays that vulgar violin of hers with distinction. But regardless of whatever instrument she happens to hold, her delicacy of expression is superior, and I only wished she would play me instead of Madeleine who tries so hard to imitate her luminosity but fails miserably, as she deserves. Madeleine deserves it, but not because she hurt me, but because her nature is a mediocre one, something I detect the moment a mediocre player lays a finger on me.

During the intermission, after a most challenging Shosta-kovich String Quartet, while I am resting and breathing hard, the same man I saw yesterday at the luthier's shop comes backstage and greets the cello player. They seem to know each other. After exchanging a few words, they walk over to where Madeleine is having her first glass of champagne and introductions take place. I cannot hear what they are saying, but all at once they look in my direction. Madeleine laughs but that man stays very serious and keeps staring at me. The three of them approach my resting place. Madeleine picks me up and hands me over to this mysterious man.

—A lovely sound. I played it yesterday at the luthier's shop.

—I'm having a hard time. I can't project well with it.

—But your phrases sound magnificent!

—You're too kind.

—How long have you had it for?

—Not long, Kiara brought it from New York last month.

—Kiara?

Madeleine breaks a conversation Kiara is having with the *Opéra* manager and pulls her toward us. The expression in Darío's face burns like petroleum when Kiara says she is happy to meet him. He almost drops me on the floor. Darío, yes, that is his name.

—Where did you get this violin?

—It's not mine; I borrowed it from a friend in New York. But Madeleine here does not like it too much.

—Well, when you're done playing, could I rehearse with it?

—My dear Darío, we've got to go back to the stage right now. Let's talk afterward.

Next comes Bartók's Fourth Quartet. The perfect opportunity. And as the concert advances, I do the best I can to sound the worse I can. I tense my ribs and firm up my belly. I keep my vibrations to a minimum. I speak in a whisper when I am supposed to scream. And when in doubt about a note, I do not compensate, I sing bravely off tune. I even conjure an old wolf tone, and I howl like an animal. For the uninitiated, the music of Bartók sounds perfectly discombobulated. But for the dedicated avantgardists, Madeleine's performance is nothing but a fiasco. If I were a famous violin, I would share in her shame. But as the lesser creature that I am, I take no responsibility.

The concert ends. The public vanishes quickly. And the conversation backstage was short and non-congratulatory. Madeleine and Kiara prepare their hasty exodus when Darío barges in once again and interrupts their plan. He convinces them to accompany him to *Les Distilleries Idéales* for a drink. The idea of Madeleine having more champagne scares me. Although she may become wretchedly unhappy with herself and consider giving me up for adoption, or maybe I could be lent out or sold again. Uncomfortable options all of them, but I am willing to accept anything to get away from her.

Les Distilleries Idéales is a place where you come to forget. People who embrace nostalgia are desperate to forget their current life. Like trading your misery for the happy memories of others. This place suits Madeleine perfectly, and with a glass of champagne in her hand, I see the magic working. But Darío seems conflicted, wanting to talk to Madeleine but wanting to drink all of Kiara at the same time. A dialectical impossibility. The first round of drinks takes place in virtually no time at all. Once they order a second round, they venture into what really matters, my destiny.

—First you wanted it, and now you hate it.

—Kiara, I really don't hate it.

—You smashed it once already.

—You know, that was an accident.

—So that's what landed it at the luthier.

—Were you there, at the luthier's shop?

—Yesterday.

—Yesterday?

—Yes, I brought my own violin because of a crack. I had a chance to play this one.

—Did it fuck with you?

—No, not really.

—Well, the bastard let me down today.

—Madeleine, you're exaggerating. I was next to you and you played very well.

—My dear Kiara, be happy about the chances you got. But I want nothing else to do with this violin.

—Easy, easy. The music was difficult to begin with.

—No, Darío, you heard how I played. I was off. Totally off.

—Well, let me play the violin for a while. Maybe we'll get along.

—Talk to her; she's the one who owns it.

—No, no, it's not mine. I have to bring it back to New York at the end of this trip.

—How long will you be around for?

—I'm not sure. I need to make some money.

—Why don't we play together?

—What do you mean?

—We can start a quartet and play contemporary stuff.

—I can't.

—Why not?

—I don't even know you.

Just when I am about to get rid of this abusive wench, they all become principled and possessive. But time is on my side. They talk some more, and they certainly drink some more. The words flow back and forth as the topics of conversation test the limits of propriety. The gazes burn holes. Darío's primarily. And by four in the morning, the three of them stumble out of *Les Distilleries Idéales* after having sowed the seed for a new string quartet. A tree that could not grow if Madeleine is to be one of its branches. But luckily for me, Darío walks away with my case in tow. I cannot tell how this happened, nor how it will end. But, for the moment, I vibrate in a perfect G sharp.

THE ARGONAUTS

When night finally falls, the cover of the oblong case closing on me, my voice fades and I could be considered mute. Time to rest now, inside this coffin, the green walls velveting me. To Darío, I might have ceased to exist. But the notes he missed or played out of tune are still in my mind, swarming like unsaid words between lovers.

Half-drunk, Darío walks away to his bedroom. Not that he intends to forget about me. He cannot. In his dreams, he pretends to play me. I hear him sometimes. He thrashes through the night searching my body with his fingers, trying to correct those notes he missed. He moans. He touches the air in the middle of the night. I pray for him not to find me then. But what good is the prayer of an inanimate soul?

I know he can destroy me anytime. It would not take much; a hard swing against the floor or against the doorframe. He could easily extinguish my voice forever. I do not like to entertain that thought. Who would like to cease to exist? But even if I fear him, I know he would not turn violent toward me. He has all of himself to be violent against. The alcohol and the self-pity already maim him. He loves me, I know, but I do not love him in return.

He turns all the lights off, except the one on the balcony outside. Not that a thief would stop at the sight of a quivering light. But maybe he feels secure that way; the same way I feel secure when he closes the lid of my case. No lights then, just the memory of a stage and the imprint of his fingers.

His main problem is one of doubt. When his fingers slide down my spine, I sense hesitation, as if he questioned where to press, where to impart that heaviness, the necessary stimulus to make me sing. Not that I sing as he wants me to sing; but that is a different matter.

Much is known about doubt, but very little understood. When his fingers land on me, poking on a precise spot on my fingerboard, I sense the intention, the very note he wants me to sing. But the smallest shift up toward the scroll of my head or down toward my belly, makes me think he is unsure. Either he does not know what he wants, or even worse, he dares to ignore me. That is when I explode, cracking the air, growing, amplifying his doubts.

At times when he grabs me, I feel his disdain, more precisely, his disgust. I, who came from nowhere, without a respectable pedigree, a mere wooden box, could make him famous, admired—even wanted. He knows I know, and that is what he despises, the sense of exposure when he is alone with me practicing. However, there are times when he surprises me with his touch when there is no pretense of music. I feel him then, and he feels me too.

Darío turns the hallway lights back on, and I hear his steps approaching. He will come to hold me, to watch how I glow in the faint light. Sometimes he licks me just to watch his saliva glistening under the light. He beholds me as a lover, my skin reflecting an amber light that excites him. All in silence, in the absence of music. I feel violated then. And during the next practice session, I turn into a dissonant beast.

That is when he plays me hard, digging the Mongol hair and roughing my cords. I sing off-tune for the very pleasure of his frustration. And I fill the air with a loud grunt, or a squeal, a screech for sure. That is when he sweats. And turning his left eye long down my neck; he wishes to strangle me.

*****

This morning he wakes up earlier than usual and snatches my case, a hard pull, swinging me away from the memory of the previous night. I know what awaits me: a long rehearsal, the ache in my ribs, his stiff fingers, and the heaviness of his breath: a mixture of red wine and over-ripe pears. Mornings like this remind me I sing for others. But even when they touch my open body, even when they rip through me, I still sing my individual harmonic frequencies. They follow the score of a dead master, but I follow my own veins. I am a violin. I count nothing musical foreign to me, so I oscillate at will, and go places they detest. Sometimes my voice is hoarse, sometimes luminous, and yet other times unreal. Who plays whom?

When we arrive at *Casa da Música*, that steel meteorite that landed in Porto at the wrong time in history, I feel a sense of foreboding. The rehearsal room is empty, and the temperature is too low for me. Kiara is not here yet. And all I want from this day is to feel her fingers, her skin. Once in a while, she sets her vulgar violin aside, places a sheet of silk between her chin and my body, and plays me—a deep, round, magnificent B flat on my G cord. I reverberate, I purr. Darío could never imagine how much I long for Kiara's fingers, not knowing, not even dreaming, that I find her touch riveting, her fingering a miracle, and her breath a mist to dive into.

But there is nobody in the rehearsal room yet. How hard to wake up in a Porto morning when a thick veil of brume hangs over you. And with the passing of the minutes, Darío becomes anxious, fidgety. When he takes me out of the case,

I fear he will start practicing alone. He does not. He simply paces back and forth and mumbles words I cannot understand. The room contains a few chairs, several music stands, and an air of sadness that sips into my belly. He begins to tap his fingers on one of the music stands, recreating a passage in Bartók's Violin Concerto No. 1. I know very well that is what he wants to play, and I am relieved he does not want to try it now.

The first to arrive is Angelo, with his beard and delicate face. When he is not distracted, he plays a good viola, which he now lays next to me as if that Venetian and I were next-of-kin. I am not related to that viola like I am not related to any antique Cremonese or any other aristocrat.

Angelo then starts talking with that soft voice of his. He tells Darío how difficult he finds his part in Bryce Dessner's *Aheym*, that he dreamt all night about his fingers getting all tied-up and his tongue swelling inside his mouth. This I find hard to imagine for his fine lips could not harbor a grotesque protruding tongue. But that is what he says, and I know Darío wants to believe all of it because he relishes anything that will make Angelo breakable.

They talk to each other with respect: a lie, a pretense. Darío wishes to be as beautiful as Angelo. When he stands in front of the mirror, playing for his imaginary audience, I know he abhors the reflected image, for his lips are not as delicate, nor his expression as virginal as that of Angelo. As for Angelo, he envies how Darío plays with such ease, such virtuosity. An unreachable dream for him, even with the help of his antique Venetian viola.

When nobody else shows up, I start to fear this will be a horrible day. Lateness can molest Darío, and he will consequently make everyone else miserable. He will play faster than necessary and criticize Leon for being over-passionate. Leon, whose smooth, rich tone is flawless. At a quarter past the hour, the room feels emptier. And the conversation between these two undeclared enemies begins to weigh on me more than the brume outside. I then concentrate on the initial notes of the *Aheym*, hoping their intensity will drown the antipathy between the earthlings. I fail. This is the difference between the sound of vocal cords and that of violin cords— the human kind can be hurtful.

Leon opens the door to the room and pushes his large case forward, sits down, and pretends to be happy. A useless attempt since they all know what delays him, that desperate need for a morning hit, an intravenous melody, the deep basso continuo of white opioids. He stays silent while unveiling his cello, placing it between his legs, and playing a few notes of the *Aheym*. I like the sound, god-like, soothing.

Without Kiara, the morning makes no sense, and the room feels desolate. I can sing with the others; I can swim through a myriad of scales. None as perfect as when her face and her long fingers come close to me though. Darío wants her too, but in a different way—a brutish way. That is why he resents those times when she puts her violin down to pick me up. His eyes go wild then, a voyeur he becomes, watching the communion of our sensual energies. He drools then; I know he drools. And I do not blame him, for when Kiara touches me, my range opens wide, and my voice reaches as far as the last row in theater heaven.

From where I am resting, I notice a watery discharge dribbling from Leon's nose as he yawns like the lion he is. I wonder if he got what he needed this morning. His watery eyes are half-closed and he continues to rehearse alone as if nobody were in the room. And he very likely feels that way, alone. But that does not keep him from playing, from trying to heal his broken reality. The day he collapsed on top of his cello, dropping his flaccid body like a rag, the fresh marks of needle punctures between his knuckles, right there for all of us to see, that day I knew he could play like a god. The sound he produced was soul-wrenching as if he had seen his last days, the confines of his very life. Leon plays music for a private reason; even if he does not know what that reason is.

When Kiara finally arrives, the round clock on the wall marks thirty minutes past the hour. Darío looks at Kiara and then at the clock, making sure she follows his gaze. He does not wait for her to set up; he simply grabs me and digs in with the Mongolian. He wants to drown her excuse in a Russian melody. I sing it, my body tense, making all the notes a little sharp. He puts me down and fiddles with my pegs, expecting to bring me back to perfect tonality. Taking pleasure in seeing him cringe, I warp his tuning efforts.

I heard Tolstoy wrote: "Happy families are all alike; every unhappy family is unhappy in its own way." And that is what I am part of: a dissonant, sad, non-rescuable, string quartet. When I see Kiara warming up by playing minor scales, while Darío makes me sing in Russian, I know our travels will not take us far today. They are called: "The Argonauts." They fight the creatures inside themselves, but they go nowhere. I wish to forget that name, "The Argonauts." One day I will.

Kiara lays her violin on an empty chair and sits with her ever-present smile spanning her face, impassive, waiting for Darío and Leon to acknowledge her arrival. Angelo has already kissed one of her cheeks. She has already touched his shoulder. And I watch as they interact with each other while Darío plays my body, wrings my neck, and usurps my sound. And I cannot help releasing a screech, a traumatic D in the fourth position of my E string, a death call, beyond the confines of harmony, making Leon stop his meditation, and forcing Darío to pull the Mongol hair away from me. I have to do this, even if it hurts me. In *Casa da Música*, despite the outside light that penetrates through the immense glass windows, we manage to find each other's darkness.

As the rehearsal gets on its way, Darío becomes excited with the initial intensity of the piece, bowing and bowing and bowing me, until all the voices coalesce into a calm bar where Leon reigns supreme. By then my body feels sore, and all I yearn is for the gentle touch of Kiara's hands, those hands that elude me.

The rehearsal grows old very soon, and soreness, like some leaden ache, descends on us all. By the time we reach the two-hour mark, Leon's dejected face speaks of a corporeal need, the tears and mucus dripping—the yawning. All at once, he stands from his stool, drops the cello on the floor, and storms out of the rehearsal room. He will not return today; I am certain he will not.

Kiara seems relieved knowing she would not have to play anymore. Angelo, however, keeps on playing, making the Venetian sing in the midst of the odd moment. He needs to prove himself, at least he thinks so. Darío takes advantage of the disarray to hold on to power. He digs into me in an effort to assert his authority. And this is when I feel assaulted, when hands make me sing for reasons other than musical virtue, when they squeeze an apocryphal voice out of my ribs.

*****

Across the street from *Casa da Música*, behind the wooden bar martyred by hard bottle edges and spilled beer, Joao waits for us to arrive. This time, only Darío and Kiara appear through the door since Leon is getting his fix somewhere out there and Angelo went home to practice some more, or maybe to cry in an empty corner. Joao, always so patient, watches as Darío and Kiara sit at a table and keep their silence. They do not speak much to each other, Darío and Kiara; they know what each other wants to say. And for that reason, they do not say anything. And the silence is the signal for Joao to approach the table and ask if they want to go heavy or light this afternoon. Kiara gestures with her hand as if petting a cat, which the waiter understands as her desire for something light. Next to her, Darío slams his fist on the table. Then Joao fetches a glass of *vinho verde* for her and a glass of tawny porto for him.

—Kiara, we're going nowhere.

—That's not true.

—We cannot even rehearse.

—I liked how Leon played.

—The junky.

—Let him be.

—Did you see his marks?

—No, I was listening to him.

—He'll kill himself.

They argue for some time while the dark and green fluids begin to exert their influence. Joao returns to the table once, twice, repeating a cycle that would numb anyone's senses. Then suddenly, they both leave the table and walk out into the street, leaving me behind, forgotten. They are only tempting fate. And fate dictates incongruent things, like Darío retracing his steps back to the bar and lifting me up with a sudden jerk on the strap of my case. Like Kiara following after him dragging her tired violin. Like both of them boarding a decrepit taxi and asking the driver to take them deep into the Ribeira where Darío's flat is certain to be waiting, dust-covered, placid, like fado in the twilight. And when the taxi stops at the curb, I hold my breath and hope for Kiara to continue the ride in the direction of her flat. This does not happen; instead, she gathers her purse, her violin, and her intoxicated brain and enters Darío's apartment building. She arrives at a new world while I enter an old story. I sense what I am about to witness, and a sick reverberation makes its way from my scroll down through my neural cords and buries deep into my belly. All the variations of the *Dies Irae* resound in my head, the Thibaud sonata, the Requiem, the Symphonie Fantastique. And as if dragged into my own funeral, Darío slogs me with his left hand, while his right hand brings Kiara up the stairs to his apartment. He drops me on the sofa with no regard for my humiliation, and he lays Kiara on the carpet right in front of me. The carnage, the vandalism is about to begin.

I hear a prelude, words I detest for their familiar ring, a chord so rich bathing my skin, and the rings of Saturn, the breath of a long horn, the resounding drum of skin-tight, and the butterflies, and the caterpillars, and the pizzicato of fractured fingers, I hear a voice woman and a voice man, the chorus of molten flesh, imprisoned flesh, and the melody of a bite, teeth puncturing, and the long, long whistling sound of air between lies. This I only hear for I do not open my eyes to the spectacle.

Darío cannot live through her. She will never let him. I wished she lived through me—an impossibility. This moment creates a sense of defeat, a realization that nothing is ever the way it ought to be. And like the lesser creature that I am, I lie prostrate on the sofa, watching as her fine hands touch the beast that plays me. And there is no music in the world that could ever drown this awareness.

*****

The Argonauts live and die by the chaos and drama they introduce into each other's lives. And the events last night, the carnage, the sexual sacrifice, will certainly prolong their dysfunctional existence. As for myself, I cannot forgive Darío, for he was the seducer, the necromancer, the beast. I will never sound the same, not in his hands, even if he plays every note perfectly. I will not vibrate kindly. I cannot.

Kiara was drunk, outlandishly drunk. That is the only reasonable explanation for her behavior. How could her hands, those hands, touch him? The image so revolting. Maybe a sense of inferiority dwells inside her mind. I think she sometimes doubts herself and her artistry. Like when she looks at the other three Argonauts after playing splendidly, still needing their nods of approval. She, who plays with true grace. Maybe because she plays second violin. Maybe that… Maybe that, compounded with the impetus of the beast, Darío, who carries on as if The Argonauts owed him their recent repute.

All I can see in front of me is the burnt battlefield. Empty. She, already gone to her place in Gaia with her violin, probably resting there and gathering a sense of reality before the rehearsal later today. And he, immersed in the vapors of his false glory. This is not where I want to be, but I have no other option but to wait until I can use my voice. They need each other as players, The Argonauts, but they need me even more, my willingness to sing, to flood the air with my voice. And Darío, more than any of them, needs me to cover his weaknesses, his imperfect intonation, his sometimes muddled phrasing. I will lie here until the afternoon rehearsal. I have enough hours to devise false notes, to concoct an alternate rhythm, to destroy the possibility of the *Aheym*.

Because life continues unaltered by those whose minds are terribly altered, because only the existence of a preternatural attraction can bring these four people together, because they could not understand their most profound symphonies, The Argonauts find themselves, once more, in the bowels of the *Casa da Música*. And after the typical prelude, where Darío imposes his ideas about the order of pieces and Leon keeps his silence, the quartet dives into their rehearsal. But instead of starting with the *Aheym*, Darío cajoles everyone to tackle Shostakovich first. I remember how this very piece dismantled Madeleine in Nice, and I hope the same will happen to Darío this afternoon. But as they play along, Darío handles me with unexpected precision and grace. I remain neutral, waiting for him to make mistakes in intonation and rhythm. He does not. Instead, he makes me sound disgustingly beautiful. Kiara's violin joins with him, and so does Leon and Angelo. Now, sounding like they have not sounded since arriving in Porto, otherworldly, like The Argonauts they aspire to be.

Kiara does not make eye contact with Darío. She stares at the sheet music and does not say a word. And when Leon yawns loudly between movements, she does not flinch. But her fingers are speaking clearly, they convey the sweetest sound ever produced from such a vulgar violin. And the fact that this miracle happens in the absence of conspiratorial gazes between her and Darío leads me to believe that she has forgotten what happened last night, or at the very least, derives no inspiration from it. This I need to believe, for I am not modifying my intentions to derail Darío from his unctuous track.

And the moment comes when the quartet takes on the *Aheym*. After the initial dense kinetic section, Leon opens with his large sound, a cathedral opening up to the sky. This I relish, his playing, his connection with something beyond himself, something that does not get destroyed by the cheap heroin he puts into his veins, into his brain. I think he could exist without the rest, alone with his sound, inside that world I do not understand. And this is the only moment in the entire piece that I will leave undisturbed. Because what is coming next will not be brilliant.

I gradually begin to unravel what should be obsessively articulated cells of energy. I simply tense my body and tighten my ribs to displace notes so slightly. And when the piece calls for lyrical and luminous lines, I sing with my roughest voice. Darío's frustration rains on me in the form of sweat. He becomes fidgety on his seat and turns to the others trying to find an explanation. Finally, he stops playing completely.

—What the fuck is going on?

Kiara and Angelo stop playing at once but Leon continues unperturbed. His eyes shut down, his mind in another world.

—What the fuck is this?

Leon descends from his cloud and looks at Darío with the most peaceful expression. Nobody answers Darío. They just swallow their words. Kiara places one of her beautiful hands on his shoulder and points at a pick-up note on the sheet music.

—Let's take it from here.

But to no avail. I do not produce a clear sound. I do not keep the tempo. And no matter how hard Darío digs in with the Mongol hair, my neural cords vibrate to my command. The piece is destroyed. Such a beautiful piece. And I feel sorry for Dessner, a talented young composer he is, but this is a personal matter that goes beyond my love for music.

—I don't understand.

—Same thing happened to Madeleine, remember?

—Do you mean I play like her?

—No, but she had a problem with this violin.

—But I haven't had any problems before.

—Easy now. Once more. From the top.

Yes, yes. Manna from the sky. Balsam for my sore sentiments. A mass for the dead. Just the opportunity I need to assert myself. Darío will not meet the harmonic challenges because I will not allow for it. And he could call out any bar number he wishes to call. He could insist on going over the same passage a hundred times. Yes, he can; but he will remain dissonant for as long as I have a voice.

The rehearsal spirals down into a dark hole from where there is no chance to recover. After many attempts to play the *Aheym* without errors, The Argonauts finally decide to stop trying. The frustration is evident in everyone's face. But no fingers are pointed, even when it is clear that Darío is the one who cannot get it right. They all fear him, they do. Maybe because he intimidates them with his words, his heavy pronouncements about correct interpretation, his philosophical take on music theory. Maybe because he is taller than every-one else, or because he can play a bastard instrument like me and still have a decent career. The Argonauts look at each other and wonder how to appear on-stage two days from now sounding like the musicians they are promoted to be.

And this brings forward the image of the pentagram. That railroad track dotted with black and white notes along the way. I have taken many trips along those tracks in times I no longer recognize. And when I merge with the notes in the tracks, my body feels whole, if feeling whole were a sentiment. And gliding along those tracks I have felt anger, jealousy, content, the desire to burn churches, a longing for lands I have never seen, like Russia or Sweden, the sense of chaos, the fear the world will decompose, a strong yearning for water, as in the sea that never ends, also a wish for death, mine, and that of others, the delusion of immortality, as if the very notes could deliver me forever forward into a non-dying state. All of this I feel when considering the pathways of the pentagram. But when I look at The Argonauts this moment, a heaviness descends on me, and I am yanked away from the music.

Kiara stores the sheet music and lays her violin inside its case. Angelo and Leon start to put everything away while Darío stays in the same position he was, disturbed, holding me tightly, wondering what went wrong, what happened to his virtuosity. He seems to understand that he failed, but cannot understand why. And his expression, that slanting of his eyes, that flattening of his smile, makes me feel like a mighty conqueror.

—We don't have any more time.

—We need at least a year.

—What's your problem, Leon?

—I don't have a problem. Does it seem like I have a problem?

—Is the juice flowing good in your veins young man?

—Let him be Darío.

—No, no… He can say whatever he wants. I played my part very well.

—Stop it now, you two.

—Kiara, the three of us played well. But Mr. Darío here didn't find his notes.

—Well, it's a challenging piece.

—Pretty face, don't try to save him.

—I'm not trying to save him. I'm trying to save us.

—Angelo, the angel.

—Enough.

At the end of the rehearsal, the torturous journey completed, The Argonauts do not go to see Joao at the bar across the street, a mistake, I think. They each part in separate ways. So, I celebrate Kiara's absence from Darío's arms, but at the same time, I long for her presence in my ambit. She will not be around me tonight. No, she will not. And I will be alone with Darío and his frustration, and his deep-rooted envy for those who play their instruments like gods. Leon plays like a god, in his mind-altered state, and so does Angelo in a purer way. And Kiara, little Kiara, she could play me like the goddess she is, she just does not know it yet.

Once at the Ribeira, in the purgatory of Darío's flat, I prepare for hell. He is quick to dump me on the floor, right in the middle of his living room. He goes to fix himself a drink and comes back to drop his body on the sofa. From that vantage point, he stares at me and I can feel the bitterness, the venom in his mind. I understand he does not really know me. How could he? He snatched me from Madeleine only a few months ago. And he has not really played me at any important venue. But in spite of our limited acquaintance, I also understand that he wishes me evil right now, that he would love to destroy me. And this is when I feel the most vulnerable, when people's idiocy threatens my very existence.

But the night is here to protect me. And all Darío manages to do in the dark is to go back and forth between the sofa and the kitchen to fetch numerous drinks and keep his blood alcohol level soaring. And every time he walks to the middle of the room where I am lying, he makes a semi-circle around me and continues walking. And every single one of these times I fear he will kick me hard and break my ribs. I am not an obstacle; he is his own obstacle. But this realization serves no purpose for he does not have the capacity for self-reflection, the brute. Deep into the night, Darío finally collapses on the sofa and screams "Apollo" at the top of his lungs.

*****

Like any other morning, this one grows from the night; but this time it promises musical blood in the afternoon, the kind that drips from the foreheads of frustrated musicians. Darío seems ready, determined to extract from me the clearest notes. He walks back and forth from the living room to the bedroom while I lie on the sofa watching him. He does not look in my direction. He simply walks and talks to himself. I remain at ease, pondering how to make him despise me, how to act so he does not act on me any longer.

At the door, the bell, and Leon materializes with a dejected expression on his face. Darío leads him to the living room where Leon sits on the sofa next to me. He is sweating, Leon is. And his arms wrap his belly while he bends over and vomits on the floor.

—Just a few euros, just a few.

—What the fuck, Leon?

—I want to play today.

—This is ridiculous.

—I've got no money.

—Fuck you, Leon. We'll get paid this afternoon.

—That's too long. I can't wait. I want to play the *Aheym* today.

—This can't go on like this.

—I've got to get the notes out.

—Get the fucking dope out. That's what you've got to do.

—I need it; I need my fix.

—Wipe your nose, will you?

—Don't be a hard ass, Darío.

—I won't do this.

—Listen, I've got the notes inside. I've got to get them out.

Darío turns away from Leon as if turning away from a leper. For a while, he continues to pace back and forth in the living room, quiet, breathing hard, as if wanting to say something important, as if wanting to swat Leon or perhaps kick him out of the flat. But he does not, he goes to his bedroom instead and returns with some cash in his hands. He lays the cash on the table and pushes it close to Leon while keeping his distance.

—Go get your shit, but you better play today.

—I'll play. It's all here, inside of me.

—I'm sure. Fuck off now.

Leon leaves with the cash in his pocket. I am sure the cash is burning, like the notes of the *Aheym* are burning inside his brain. I know he will show up at the *Casa da Música* later today. He has to show up. The musical notes burn at a higher temperature than the heroin notes. He may feel the oozing pain of heroin withdrawal, but the pain of not playing his cello hurts deeper. He leaves now, a little boy running, and Darío watches him as he skips down the stairs without looking back, leaping into a state of joy that only addicted Leon can comprehend. I never saw a drug addict before, with that massive need to get their fix, but looking at Leon, I come to realize how real that need is, how immense.

*****

The sinusoidal ramps outside *Casa da Música* invite a vast array of drifters. Skateboarders of all ages, observers who wish to do what the skateboarders do, and others who simply admire the curves erupting from the ground. The building stands there, in the middle of the mayhem, pretending to be a beacon of culture in this old town that drips pale tears in the humid sadness of the Atlantic. And into this fallen meteor I enter, dragged by Darío, expecting the most phenomenal performance from The Argonauts. This is no longer a rehearsal; this is where we shine or where we face our doom.

But I will not permit The Argonauts to perform at their best. I know I could sing beautifully, but not in Darío's hands. He needs to be punished. I am not a judge, and I am not a vigilante, but I could only sing my best in the hands of those who believe in me. Darío believes in himself, only in himself. All he does is drool over Kiara and pretend to be the honest man he is not. And I despise him on both accounts.

Inside Sala Suggia, the air feels crisp; unlike the sultry brume bathing Porto this afternoon. I can sing on this stage, and my voice would carry to the furthest corners of the room. The Nordic pine on the walls and the curved glass will make my notes levitate, especially my high notes. And then there is the light, the unearthly luminosity making the room expand as if the sky had entered the room. I feel absolute inside Sala Suggia. A wooden box inside a meteoric box, a voice inside a silence, an amnesic bastard inside a royal palace. Not an inferiority complex, but a reality, my state in this world is such. And I will be heard today, by whom I am yet to discover, but I will be heard.

Angelo arrives, Kiara arrives, yes, and a little later Leon makes his entrance in complete composure, his hands steady, his eyes open, his nose dry. We all gather inside the little room behind the Sala Suggia. My fellow instruments are unearthed from their cases as we prepare to rehearse a few difficult passages. The words between The Argonauts are scarce, nothing but the essential, not a salutation, no kindness. And the first command comes from Darío who, with a swift gesture and a sharp inhale, leads the way into the first few bars of the *Aheym*. This goes on for a few lines only until Darío redirects the quartet toward Bartók's String Quartet No. 3. Here we pause to infuse the piece with space, air, and meaning. I feel perfectly fine, vibrating smoothly, warming up for what is to come. Darío then signals a sudden stop to the rehearsal and begins to talk.

—Amédée is coming to the concert.

—How do you know?

—They told me at the reception.

—So what?

—Leon, don't be an idiot.

—I play the way I play. I don't care who's out there.

—Play better then.

—You play better, Darío.

—I will if this bastard cooperates.

—The old man blaming the violin.

—No, I'll blame you if you fuck up.

—What do you think, Angelo? Can the old man here play any better?

—Drop it. Enough!

—Listen to Kiara. She knows.

Yes, she often knows, but I do not understand why she touched Darío with those hands. Even worse, why did she let him touch her? She should know better. The hands that play me are the same hands that give pleasure. The hands that lift a glass of wine are the very same hands that press on my fingerboard. They cannot be separated. All the hands playing a handless being like myself. I may be at the mercy of the hands of others, but my voice is different; it is at the mercy of nobody, nobody.

The composer, Amédée, is here to listen to my voice and the voices of the Venetian viola, the vulgar violin, and Leon's cello. He is not here to listen to Darío; he is certainly not. And if he were to compose a piece for The Argonauts, as unlikely as that may be, it would be because of our voices, not because of The Argonauts' hands. But if I were to sing in a manner of distinction, Darío would go unpunished. And if I were to derail the performance, Amédée would never hear my voice again. One way or another, I will be heard today.

I observe the audience populating the Sala Suggia, centipedes crawling amid rows of seats, hushed voices, the ruffle of pamphlet pages, and I hear the voice of a man speaking in Portuguese announcing the appearance of The Argonauts. We take the stage, and the audience, palm against palm, celebrate our entrance with unearned enthusiasm since we have yet to play a single note. Whether they will clap in the same manner after finishing our performance is a mystery. All I know is that this performance will be memorable.

At this moment the curtains are parted, unveiling the expansive window behind the stage. The trees in the *Jardim da Boavista* come to sit among the audience, and a misty light floods the interior of the Sala. And from the edge of this instant, looking over the musical paradise about to unfold, I feel the weight of a thousand ambitious instruments that came before me, their vibrations, tonalities, highs and lows, a lineage of desperate wooden boxes reaching back to the crib in Cremona.

We start. Our neural cords begin to vibrate, all at once, in the opening phrases of the *Aheym*. The sound crashes against the glass walls, against the bodies and faces of the audience, and the air in the Sala boils with a sense of urgency, and the theme bounces from one wooden box to another, and the unanimous wave of musical notes grows, impregnating the far corners of the Sala, when all at once the music stops for one *pausa de semínima*, after which Leon ascends from his narcotic stupor, a phoenix, a most splendorous bird, transforming the minds of The Argonauts who play as if they loved each other, in a trance, and so on until the last note of the *Aheym*.

The audience erupts in ovation. My body trembling, my cords aching, I watch Angelo's beautiful face, Kiara's delicate hands, and Leon's lost gaze. It is not them who I need to shatter; it is only Darío. We are just at the beginning of the performance; we still have pieces from Bartók and Philip Glass. I need to calm down, recuperate, descend from the heights of resplendence, and fix my attention on the task of destruction.

We proceed to play Philip Glass's Quartet No. 5, and again, I fall for the minimalistic beauty. The simplicity and purity inherent to the piece generate a sense of intimacy with my fellow instruments, and for the entire duration of the piece, I forget about the hands that play us all. The brotherhood of our bodies, grounded in spruce and maple, our shapes, our resonance, our carved openings, all our components sourcing a sound from a time before this time. And facing each other in this semi-circle opened to the audience, we relate in ways that go beyond the actuality of this moment. We vibrate, and in so doing, we feed from each other, consuming, bar after bar, the totality of Mr. Glass's spirit.

The intermission finds me gasping, ecstatic from the exquisite resonance of the Sala. And once in the little room again, Darío lays me inside my case and leaves the cover open, a move I appreciate for I need to breathe the air still pregnant with our voices. He quickly steps up to greet Amédée, who makes his entrance into the room with a benevolent expression on his face. To imagine that he would consider composing an exclusive piece for The Argonauts is outside the realm of my expectations, even when I consider myself a unique voice. Yes, I consider myself unique, a unique bastard. The two of them talk, then Kiara joins them, then Angelo approaches them and smiles a nervous smile. Leon stays by himself in the corner of the room where he plays a few notes on his cello, his eyes closed, his mind probably searching for a place outside this reality.

I cannot tell the words they exchange, but they must have been significant because Kiara kisses Amédée on his cheek before returning to pick up her violin. Darío comes over and lifts me out of the case with a sudden jerk that rattles my body. Angelo then holds the viola in his left hand and leads the way back into the Sala where the audience is waiting for us, on their feet, clapping as if we were gladiators about to take on a beast. And I share the feeling, for I am about to dismember the most beautiful composition from Bartók. If good came from our performance in the first half of this concert, I am happy to take responsibility for my part. And if bad is to come from the second half, I am to blame. I already showed what my voice can do. That is enough! I now need to dislodge Darío from my life. Not because he cannot play me well, but because he touched Kiara.

Not everything that starts well ends well. The *prima parte* in Bartók's composition flows with grace, solidifying Darío's confidence and building on his success from the first half of the program. He must be happy with himself; I feel it in the assertive bowing. I think his playing impressed Amédée; I am sure it did. But I can prove that it was my voice, our voices, and not his playing. So, as we embark on the *seconda parte*, the Allegro, I tense my body, refusing to vibrate, crippling the sound, bringing the mighty Darío to his knees. He presses harder on my cords, trying to make me sing louder. I resist and tense my body even harder. I fear I may crack, but I tense every single fiber of my body as hard as I can. The contrapuntal adventure comes apart, the dance-like melody assumes a ghostly cadence, and the audience begins to murmur.

*****

From the interior of the café, through the open door facing the Douro, I marvel at the constant drizzle and reminisce of Venice in June. A time now gone forever, it seems. The waters of the Douro flow fast, and I feel like joining them. Darío's arm weighs heavy as he leans on me to get his legs on top of the center table, tilting the chair back and sipping still more tawny. Kiara also looks out the door, and I wonder if she admires the water falling from the sky or the one sourcing the river. They are one and the same, different phases in their lives, that is all.

How many shades of gray could the afternoon light reveal? Countless. How many musical tones could Kiara's fingers evoke in me; beyond countless. She remains quiet, simply admiring the beauty that unfolds in front of her. Maybe she thinks of another world, of another life. Maybe she wants to be quiet to preserve the melody of the waters. I am content with being quiet, with not having to spoil any more concerts. And somehow, I think that explains this interlude; a time and place between battles on the stage. Here, where the only melody is the one of water.

The sound of steps down the adjacent street punctures the gray peace. Syncopated steps, determined. And within a few seconds, the figure of a man blocks the door to the café, and the gray light and the falling rain are no longer. And when the man makes his way into the café, I immediately recognize the bare face and the red hair of the little devil. Kiara steps up and greets him with a warm embrace. Darío gets his feet off the table, pushes me to the side, and barks a few words I cannot understand. He approaches the little devil and shakes his hand with unnecessary force. And before Kiara has the chance to say anything, Darío introduces himself and starts talking about Porto and its dreadful weather.

—The rain, the constant drizzle. All because of this unnerving coast. And the wind. Yes… the wind.

—I feel the cold. The humidity also claws at me. For how long have you lived here?

—Too long.

—Are you planning to go elsewhere?

—I don't have an answer to that question.

—Well, Kiara says she wants to go back to New York.

—Is that right?

Kiara abandons the view of the flowing river and turns her attention to the conversation between Darío and the little devil. She places her soft right hand on Darío's shoulder and pushes him down until he has no chance but to sit and take a servile position. She then hands me over to the little devil who recognizes me at once.

—Here it is, my friend from the jazz club.

—Do you remember its sound?

—Totally.

—Then play something.

—Right now?

—Yes, play something for me.

The little devil takes the bow strapped inside the cover of my case. He then erupts into a solo, grouping the notes in dotted pairs with a subtle and constantly changing emphasis. He swings, and when I try to guess what note he will play next, he moves up or down the scale. He lengthens and shortens notes so that the accent comes *off* rather than *on* the beat, creating surprise and a sense of urgency. Like this, he soars in front of Darío's eyes, endearing Kiara, and making me feel like I matter, even if I matter little in comparison with the miracle of his improvisation.

Just when I am getting ready to deepen the adventure, he stops playing and pushes me aside. I do not like being tossed around this way. Once I start to feel the music, once the fibers in my body vibrate in unison, I yearn for more, my voice looking to flood the space around me. Well, that does not happen. I find myself lying supine away from any of the fingers that could bring me to life. The little devil takes Kiara's fingers among his own fingers and plays with them, feeling their delicate contours, their exquisite length. Darío brings his hands together, interlaces his own fingers, and in blatant disregard for his brutality; he hyperextends every single one of his phalanges making the most unsavory crackling sound.

—You call that jazz.

—I don't call anything jazz.

—But you're improvising.

—Says who?

—You're improvising.

—I just play the notes that need to be played.

—Isn't that improvisation?

—No, it's a need.

—But whose need is it?

—I don't know.

—Well, it must be your own need.

—Maybe you're right, but maybe the violin wants me to play it that way.

—The violin?

—Yes, the violin.

—This bastard has no sense of itself.

—How do you know it's a bastard?

—Look for yourself.

—I don't need to. I'm already familiar with it.

—No label. Nothing. And the sound…

—I don't trust labels, but I trust the sound.

—Indeed, it sounds horrible.

—Not in my hands.

—Well, I'm deeply disappointed with it.

—Disappointed?

—Yes, deeply.

—Then, let me have it. I don't mind playing it.

—I don't really own it, Kiara does.

—I don't think Kiara is the owner either.

—Really? Kiara, whose violin is this?

She does not answer. And instead of her words, I hear the collision of Darío's disappointment and the little devil's urgency to possess me. I hear the sound of Kiara's liquid dreams and her petrified sadness. I hear the voices that keep ringing in my ears, through the centuries, unabated, questioning my ascendency and my rightful place in a player's hands. And I hear all of this instead of music, and I want to scream, out of tune, and tear the air in the process.

The three of them eventually sit down and manage to carry on a conversation about the rain. They order another round of drinks. When Darío and the little devil appear to be comfortable with each other, Kiara takes advantage of the momentary truce and steps out of the café. Without an umbrella, without inhibition, she begins to dance under the rain, under the leaden Porto sky. The water falling, Kiara's hands rising and falling, the afternoon hours falling, all the grays falling to the ground, and the ground falling deep into itself.

Inside the café, Darío talks incessantly while the little devil remains quiet and watches Kiara through the open door. And the more Darío talks, the more profoundly the little devil observes Kiara's wet figure. He must be dying. He must be feeling what I feel when she plays me. Precipitously, he emerges from the trance and lifts my body again. And with the fluidity of mercury, he begins to play me. He glides into a melancholic improvisation, dark, haunting, and my voice falls endlessly into a deep lament. Kiara hears my voice and begins to turn and turn as if her body obeyed my every whisper. I sing under the spell of the little devil's darkness, and Kiara dances under the spell of my voice. And the rain keeps on falling, falling.

Wet and eternal, Kiara steps back into the café, and with her eyes closed, she holds the little devil's hands and stops his playing. As she stands on a puddle made by her dripping dress, she keeps humming the chord progression I was just singing while adding nuances of her own. And I wish I could join her. If I could sing on my own, I would this very moment.

Darío stands up and raises his glass of tawny. He makes a shallow bow and drinks the entirety of the glass. The little devil lets go of Kiara's hand and grabs two glasses. He offers one to Kiara and the other he keeps for himself. And as if there was nothing else in this world but the presence of wet Kiara, the little devil brings the glass to his lips and drinks his tawny as if he was drinking life. The liquid enters his body, the water dripping from Kiara's dress enters his mind, and the water falling down on the streets of Porto enters his consciousness, as it has already entered into mine. And I know we share the same object of desire, the little devil and I.

The glasses of tawny keep arriving at our table, the wrath of the liquid keeps on pounding the delicate brain cells of the trio, and the rain keeps on pounding the gray sidewalk. I fear for them as I fear for the leather in drums, beaten, stretched, giving out because they have to. And I wonder if Darío has to fail, if the little devil has to marvel at his own marvel, and if Kiara has to play a second violin when she could play me in front of the world, with her delicate hands, making me sing like the venerated princes of Cremona. But this moment is not the moment for wondering. Darío gets up from his chair, wobbles, and reaches out for my neck. Kiara slaps his hand. He continues his deliberate reach, and Kiara slaps his hand again with more force. He drops his hands to the side of his body, and he whines. I think he cries.

The little devil ignores the interaction. He lights a cigarette and proceeds to smoke with his eyes shut. He then starts to hum a tune unknown to me, melancholic, maybe gray. He moves his head side-to-side while humming this tune. And when Darío falls on the floor, drunk and dejected, the little devil keeps on humming the tune, unmindful of anything else. Kiara sits next to him and tries to follow the music singing in falsetto. But when she manages to imitate the melody, the little devil changes the tune.

*****

The first few notes point in the direction of the sky. I know where this composition is going. It will ascend, in a pyramidal way, from a broad base to the small point at the apex, and from there it will take flight; or it will all come crashing to the ground. After the second dissonant start, Darío gestures for everyone to stop. There is no talk. And with another abrupt gesture, the music resumes.

Amédée seems a little worried as he listens to The Argonauts give his composition a first run. He does not sit down for a second; he keeps walking around the rehearsal room as if considering the music from every possible angle. He stops at the furthest corner of the room and kneels on the floor facing the wall. There he starts to weep. Darío gestures again and the music stops. The suffocating weeping is loud. And without turning his head, Amédée requests for us to go on while he continues to weep in the corner.

The first movement makes me think of the ocean, as a feeling of universal belonging spills out of my belly. But, as the next movement ensues, The Argonauts fail to play their best. The wonderful piece does not take flight. The crashing is sobering, and we all know it. Leon is the first to walk out of the room with his head down. Kiara looks up to the ceiling while Darío squeezes my neck so hard I feel he will break me. Amédée remains in his corner, oblivious to what we are doing, the weeping now less pronounced. Nobody talks but the silence.

Outside the *Palau de la Música*, the narrow streets of the *Barri Gótic* boil with life and energy and nobody there is aware of our failure. Nobody else will become aware because once played in the rehearsal room, the dreadful notes vanish, leaving no trace. Our collective memories retain a relic of the failure, but those memories are being destroyed this very minute. When Amédée finally gets up from his knees and faces Darío, the two men exchange a moment of defeat. They agree to try again tomorrow as if tomorrow would indeed be a different day.

After everyone has left, alone now, Darío comes around and stands in front of my case. Exhausted after the fiasco at the rehearsal, I lie on my back, my belly exposed, my f-holes breathing hard. He seems intent on staring at me as if I have something to say. He does not move, nor does he say a word; he just stares at me. I fear him when he does this. He already hates me, and his mind is all wrapped around his frustration. He grabs me by the neck with both hands. My bottom points up to the ceiling. He squeezes hard, and I feel my neural cords pulling through my bridge down to my endpin. He is going to hurt me. He swings me hard through the air. He swings me even harder, and my ribs crack a little. And when he takes another hard swing at the air, my body starts to vi-brate inconsolably, oozing a deep tone that fills the room. I am singing from the very core of my wood, the primal fibers crying a primal fear. Darío swings at the air again, and my sound grows even larger, a basso continuo, a fearful yearning from my very essence, grown and created centuries ago in unknown hills by unknown hands.

Rabid, Darío lays me on the floor as if I was a venom-ous serpent. He sits on a chair, covers his ears with both hands, and starts to rock back and forth, forth and back, at the rhythm of my vibrations. We stay like this for a while, our bodies oscillating, responding to each other, until the air particles attenuate their movements, and we enter a silence—a moment of peace. We both feel exhausted. I know I do. He fears failure while I fear for the integrity of my wood. Both fears are elemental, felt at the very core of the self. For Darío, the recognition of his capacity as a premier player is vital; for me, the capacity to vibrate like no other violin is life.

Our days in Barcelona crawl slowly, and our progress mastering Amédée's piece finds a genuine deadness. We meet every morning at the rehearsal room of the *Palau*, and every morning we walk out of that room with fresher doubts about ourselves. The Argonauts argue, the travels ahead are disputed, the boats are sunk, and the dreams are quickly forgotten. The music, that ethereal arrangement of sounds and emotions, begins to lose tangibility, like fog at midday. By this time, Amédée has stopped attending the rehearsals. He finds excuses that oblige him elsewhere.

*****

This morning, Leon walks into the rehearsal room and refuses to play a single note. He does not even take the cello out of its case. He is not high, and he is not withdrawing either. He simply stands there, his arms crossed over his chest, looking at the rest of The Argonauts. Darío wants to start the rehearsal, but Leon does not move. And neither Kiara nor Angelo, say anything. Darío takes me out of the case and starts to play his part alone, ignoring everyone else.

—That's the problem.

—What's the problem, Leon?

—That you think you're God.

—I do what needs to be done.

—Then drop that violin.

—What do you mean?

—I mean you drop that violin and let Kiara play it.

—Kiara plays a second violin very well.

—No question about that. You're the question.

—What are you talking about?

—She'll play a better first violin.

—And who's so sure about that?

—The music.

The music speaks, it debates, and at the end, it conjures the hands that need to come into being. The music demands for every fiber of ourselves to engage in the process of creation. The music demands the best from us. And Leon knows what I know, and what Darío wants to ignore: that I have a better chance at fulfilling Amédée's vision in the hands of Kiara. But Leon is Leon, so he dons a cloak of silence after his brave speech. Darío continues to play his part, and he is eventually joined by the three others. And the rehearsal today ends like it did yesterday—nowhere.

Friday comes and it brings a burning sensation, an uncomfortable warmth for a Friday in February among the frigid buildings of the *Barri Gótic*. As we wait for Amédée to come into the rehearsal room, very little is said. Angelo taps the back of his viola, and the sweet melody seems to soothe him. But no one else responds, and the melody goes unnoticed. In the background, I distinguish the low belch of a tuba practicing for the concert tonight. A full orchestra will take the stage—many more instruments to blame in such grand arrangements. For a string quartet like ours, hell is more tangible, more intimate.

Then comes Amédée with his face burning like the Friday of the day, empty-handed, without any sheet music. A redness covers his skin and his eyes are wide open, unblinking, staring at each of The Argonauts. He comes over to my case, lifts me up, and feels my spine. And as he starts to play the first bar of his composition in a deliberate pizzicato, I sense a disquiet energy, like when rain falls on a hot roof. He continues to play me a little longer until he stops at once.

—This is my music. This is what I intended.

—We're almost there. We just need a few more days.

—Darío, what keeps you from mastering this?

—I'm having a hard time with the violin.

—The violin doesn't lie. You just heard me playing it.

—You're right; the violin doesn't lie.

—I wrote the piece for this violin.

—Well, it's not sounding well.

—The composition or the violin?

—The violin.

—Let Kiara play it, then.

The words fall into a deep abyss. Darío keeps his eyes fixed on Amédée but does not respond. Kiara closes her eyes and squeezes the body of her violin until her knuckles turn white. And the burning sensation of the day Friday grows, inundating the room, making the air heavy.

—Let's not discuss that now, Maestro.

—Kiara, do you have an opinion?

—Yes, Maestro.

—What is it?

—The violin doesn't lie.

—You're right. It's a very honest violin.

I sound the only way I can. I simply flower. Sometimes

the notes come out obtuse, perhaps dissonant, but that is not on purpose, it is just another way to interpret what the composers had forgotten to explore. Not all is apparent in the pentagram, much remains to be excavated. So, when the players massage my cords, only a guiding whisper I hear, for my body needs to feel the urges and vibrate at will. Death is a melody predicted. Death is when the pitch and diction of the phrases sound like well-known echoes, a stale memory. Death is a repeated story. I dare to go astray from the pentagram but with creative impetus. I do not attempt to adulterate the canon with alternative phrases. I do not reinvent. In reality, I resonate with the same materials as any other violin. But my wood is my wood, and my cords cross my body on a personal angle.

I need to be liberated, released. And Amédée may have intuited my needs when he wrote this piece for us, The Argonauts. And, unknowingly, he may destroy us. Or perhaps he may help us transcend. We need a private revolution, an internal coup. But the heavy hand of Darío suffocates me. And the more he wants me to please Amédée, to sing by prescription, the more distant we get from the truth. If there is a truth, it is found in music. And if there is honesty, it is found in my inner vibrations. So, I revolt and sing my song, bringing the day Friday to full combustion.

Through the *Barri Gótic* we walk, away from the shame and disappointment. The Argonauts, a foursome without force. And we walk aimlessly, directionless, just walking away. Inside my case, I feel the incessant banging of Darío's thigh against my flank. And the force of the banging surpasses the rhythm of the walk, and I fear for the later hour. The walking rhythm comes to a stop at an empty plaza surrounded by decrepit buildings where the voices of The Argonauts bounce from wall-to-wall. They sit around a table on questionable wooden chairs that exhale when their bodies mold over them. I feel for the wood of these chairs. The Argonaut's words travel from mouth to mouth, and I avoid interpretation. I only think of Bach and the sense of a universal emotion, an oceanic experience, a shared musical existence. And somehow, I know we are wounded.

Dragging instrument cases around the streets of Barcelona is not a travesty, but sitting down at a café in a medieval plaza and not ordering drinks is outrageous. So the alcohol is sure to flow. And it does. The first drinks are paid by Darío who wants to secure his position as leader of the quartet, or at least, as the originator of events, drinking, musical, or otherwise. But before the first glasses are consumed, Leon takes leave and disappears through a small street leading somewhere behind the plaza. He does not say goodbye, nor does he take his cello with him. He needs a fix, and the rest of The Argonauts know it. I wonder how much influence dope exerts on his playing. I may never know, but if touching God makes you play like Leon plays, then heroin must be the very finger of God, slightly bent, like the finger of the God in the Sistine Chapel.

Nobody else joins them at the plaza, only glasses of alcohol arrive which get quickly consumed. Their voices continue to attack the brick walls of the buildings. And the harder the voices hit those walls, the harder they bounce back. And they hear themselves, the offending voices, the purgatory voices. I try to find musical notes in those voices, even in the softer register of their speech, but what I hear is not music; what I hear is an elegy. Kiara's voice in particular, sounds low and broken. Her hands do not emit dark tones, so it must be her mind doing the talking. Her hands levitate, touching nothing, or maybe the air.

—Maybe if I change the strings…

—No, Darío, it's not about the strings.

—But you heard how it sounded.

—It's not about the strings.

—Then what is it, Kiara?

—I don't know.

Kiara sits up on her chair and pulls my case towards her. She picks me up and turns to face Darío. And without averting her eyes away from his, she starts to play the first bars of Amédée's composition. I relax and let my body vibrate with amplitude. I inhale deeply and exhale the purest notes into the empty plaza. The music resonates, bouncing against those same walls, but returning without vengeance. Leon emerges from the back streets with a calm expression on his face. He sits next to Kiara and places the cello between his legs. He plays a few notes, pauses, closes his eyes, and continues to play his part of the composition. The notes caress each other, ascend high over the buildings and spill over the roofs. The hands, Kiara's hands, and my voice are one. I simply let go. She leads. I sing through her hands. And for the first time, Amédée's composition sounds as intended, but there is no Amédée to witness the miracle.

—Enough, enough!

Darío pulls me away from Kiara, from her hands. He dumps me inside the case and slams the cover. A deep dull pain stabs me. He may have cracked my back.

—Fuck all of you!

Once again, I feel the incessant banging of Darío's thigh

against my flank as he walks away from the plaza. The brutal force of the banging increases as he walks faster and faster. And my back feels the later hour approaching, and I fear the hurt.

*****

In the company of the dead, in the company of the moribund, the frustrated, the desecrated, in the company of unreason, obstinacy; in such company I find myself at this late hour. Darío, comatose, and obtuse, lies next to me on the floor of the hotel room. The profane globe of his stomach rises from the floor. If he vomits now, he would die looking at the ceiling.

The air filters through the windows bringing noises from the street; children, animals, mopeds. Together those scattered notes compose an original music, the music of Barcelona in the morning. Every town has its own music. It changes throughout the day, hour by hour. But a certain sentiment remains, a theme. People in the town compose the music unknowingly by walking, talking, dragging their pets and children; making love. To the virgin, the amalgam of sounds may seem like noise; a brutal concoction served raw. But once the nuances are understood, once the delicacies of every whisper burr under your skin, there is no longer noise, but a music worthy of the gods.

My listening, living, and dreaming of the notes Amédée composed gets interrupted by a sudden knock on the door. Whoever is knocking must be hurting, for the pounding on the hard wood is hard. And between one arpeggio of crashed fingers and the next, I hear the deep breath of a deep soul, a yearning, a thirst. Darío does not open his eyes. He turns on his side, and the globe of his abdomen wants to burst and spill all over the floor, but the tight skin keeps it in place. The knocking continues until Darío screams.

—The door is open!

Yes, it is open. And Leon plows into the room disturbing the music of Barcelona in the morning. His nose is dry, his pupils normal in size. He seems fixed, or at least safe from withdrawal. He comes close to the recumbent Darío and kneels on the floor. Without saying a word, he observes Darío for a few seconds, long enough to surmise the ruin in front of him. He pokes Darío's abdomen with his finger. No answer. He pokes him again. Darío opens his mouth, but no sound comes out. Just a breath, if anything.

—I know you can hear me. You're not dead. I have to do this. I have to take that violin away from you. You're not playing well.

—Leon…

—Don't say anything.

—Wait…

—There's no waiting. I'm taking it with me.

Leon gets up from the floor and comes over to the sofa where I lie in anticipation of a coup d'état. He grabs my case, swings the strap over his shoulder, and turns to head for the door. But he finds Darío standing in the way, the mountain of his body raised from the floor, a hovering mass, eyes with red rivers, and both arms extended with the palms flat against the air.

—Leave that violin here.

—No, you cannot play it.

—Leave that violin here, I'm telling you.

—Just accept it, Darío.

—She's not going to play it.

—Who?

—Kiara. She's not going to get her hands on it.

—Even Amédée suggested it.

—She's not touching it.

Leon tries to move fast around the mass of Darío's body. But when he is about to clear the way, Darío snatches the strap of my case and yanks it with all his force. The tug snaps the case from Leon's shoulder and sends it flying in the air. As my case crashes on the floor, the impact throws me out of it, and I come to rest naked on the floor, facing down, pivoting on my bridge. A wrong move from either of them and I would be crushed, finished.

—Get out of here. Go and shoot up that shit.

—Nothing's going to change, Darío.

—What do you know?

—I know you have no chance.

—Neither does she.

—You heard her at the plaza. She can play this violin.

—But she won't.

Leon could easily manhandle Darío and extricate me by force. But no battle ensues, he simply reaches for the door and leaves. And as he strides down the narrow streets of the *Barri Gòtic*, I hear him whistle the first movement of Amédée's composition.

THE ABUSE

I do not mind traveling by train, seeing the terrain as it passes by. I belong to those pine forests. I belong to their eternal green unaltered by the seasons. That I never forget, my belonging. But traveling by plane, when I am stuffed inside a little coffin on top of people's heads, in close proximity with those who know nothing about music and are ready to push their chattel against my case, with no view to enjoy; that is hell, a hell I want to forget.

When we enter one of those small planes and Darío opens the overhead compartment, all I hope is for a short-lived hell. Where we are going in this abrupt trip, I do not know; but the solitude surrounding Darío scares me. The dry air inside this flying machine makes my joints crack. It then takes me more than a day to recover my natural moisture. I was not meant for this. I was meant for slow travel in close contact with the earth.

The spoken words from the passengers sound far away. I try to understand what they say, but everything becomes a senseless chatter. There is no music here, only the continuous humming of the engines, the brutal utterance of the machine. I wish I could hear the air as it flows and twirls around the wings of the machine. That makes wonderful music, the music of the sea eagle. But inside this hermetic coffin, all I barely distinguish is the voice of the captain, a louder voice but still unintelligible.

After about one hour, the machine drops from the sky and I feel it landing on the ground. Everything moves. The bag beside me leans hard against my case. I tense my fibers and wait for the turmoil to subside. Many words are spoken, and the hands of the crowd open the coffins, and the chattel is unearthed with no consideration or sentiment. Darío finally pulls me out of this hell, and we descend a stair which brings us into an openness where the sea and the sky flirt with each other and a salty breath drenches us.

This is the Mediterranean Sea, unmistakable. These are its blues and its familiar wind flutes. This is Nice, between the mountains and the sea, between two distant layers of memory. I was hurt here by Madeleine. And here I first sang for Darío when I did not yet know his kind. He impressed me with his skills. "Lark Ascending," I remember. I flew then. But coming here unexpectedly, without the rest of The Argonauts, without a scheduled concert, seems ominous.

After a short taxi ride, we arrive at *Les Distilleries Idéales* where Darío sits at a quiet table and pretends to read the paper. His eyes move from the paper to the door, to the paper, to the door, and so on. This is where he kidnapped me. That is exactly what he did. And if he returns to the same place, it must be for an equally sinister reason. He must expect Madeleine to fall prey to another of his maneuvers. Why else would he bring me here? To return me to her? I doubt that. In the background, I hear a tune that reminds me of eunuchs. I have never met a eunuch, but the music paints such an image in my mind. They call it "pop," this music.

And as I expected, Madeleine arrives with a violin in tow. She sits at the table and orders a glass of champagne. If champagne was a problem at the end of a concert two years ago, it must be worse at the beginning of this questionable interlude. She leans over me, takes a good look, and smiles. And from the angle where I repose, I see her teeth, her inept hands, and I shiver. Regardless, she seems happy to meet Darío, not me. I am sure of that.

They converse. They look at each other. They open the case of the violin Madeleine brought with her. Darío takes the violin in his hands and touches the exposed body, irritating the poor thing. He does not try to make it sing, not now at least. They talk some more. Over the course of an hour, Madeleine has three more glasses of champagne, and I sense she is reaching a level field with Darío. They ignore me, which I greatly appreciate. And for two people that do not know each other that well, they seem too intimate; each with their agenda.

Madeleine cannot help herself; she stares at me from the edge of her chair, and I know this day will cause a commotion.

—Do you like playing it?

—It gets better and better.

—What are you working on?

—A piece by Amédée. He composed it exclusively for us.

—How lucky!

—Yes, but… we're struggling.

—How so?

—I don't understand it myself.

—The music?

—No, the violin.

This admission of weakness, this tenderness, cannot be genuine. He wants to manipulate this woman. Why would he insist on coming to this very place where, in their last encounter, she gave me away? She hated me. I know that. And now Darío does not stop talking to her, and she listens. I wonder what they really think. They connect with each other on some devious level. Maybe their respective doubts bind them together. And after several drinks, they reach that point when both agree on everything. So, they decide to go to the *Opéra* and play me.

The road, paved with falsities, leads to the *Opéra de Nice* where inside a rehearsal room I find myself in the hands of Darío while Madeleine is raising the violin that she brought along with her. Under the single chandelier that hangs in the center of the room, they start playing. They exchange phrases. Notes from Sibelius Concerto in D minor emanate from Madeleine's violin, and the clarity impresses me, for I remember the last time when she failed me. Or was it me who failed her? Darío makes me sing Schoenberg Op. 36. And I agree to be played, and I do it well. Then Berg, "To the Memory of an Angel." Perhaps I am singing to my memories, those I cannot remember. Perhaps I am resurrecting those days that belong to my forgotten past. Madeleine responds with a Grieg sonata. And one phrase touches another, and they interweave, and they fill the corners of the room. The resonance of my voice, impregnated with desire, bounces back from the walls and penetrates my body. This is when I sing my best, when there is a rapture. I become myself, but richer, deeper.

Darío, now bold and pro-pulsed by the mystery of the stunning sound, embarks in the sublime journey of the Bach Sonata for Violin Solo No.1. Madeleine stops playing and quiets her violin. I seize the moment and modulate my voice, creating spaces between notes to occupy the universe. The entire human existence is contained in this sonata, all the love, the hatred, the fear, and aspirations of every woman and man that once lived and those that are yet to live. Alone I sing, and then I whisper. And the room disintegrates, the walls falling, the roof caving, the entire Opéra building collapsing. In front of us the sea, vast. Behind, the mountains stand.

A silence grows, and we find ourselves in its center. Madeleine with her violin by her side, Darío still holding me tight. The world pausing. No memories now, just a silence without time. A moment without music. I recognize the potential to incarnate a different being, to flourish from inside my body as another. But I do not. My voice, quiet now, is who I am and will be. So here I rest, in a plenitude derived from Bach immortal. Even when Darío's hands could degrade me, torture me even, I will remain impassive in the center of this silence.

And, one-by-one, the walls begin to ascend. The stones climb each other in a fever to recreate the rehearsal room as we knew it. The ceiling covers the sky, and the wooden floor covers the ground. The chandelier hangs itself in the center of the room. And the four of us assume the playing position choreographed centuries ago. And ripping through the air, a G sharp delivers time again.

Everyday contains a moment when we think we have touched immortality. What follows next is the stuff of life. And the life I have to live is about to change once more. Madeleine reaches for me, and Darío lets me go with such ease, with a gesture as ancient as the first abandonment. I am handed over, transferred once more. She must remember how I unraveled her concert and made her look amateurish. But now, she must believe I am an angel who can sing and stop time.

—But what about this violin that you don't understand? It sounds wonderful.

—It does, this moment it does.

—I couldn't make it sound that way when I had it.

—Neither can I.

—But you just did.

—It seems like I did.

Darío steps back and stares at Madeleine, who stands in the middle of the room holding me. Disbelief deforms his face, and his arms drop like rags on the side of his body, disheartened now. He moves forward as if to reach for me, perhaps with the intention of grabbing me away again. But he stops when Madeleine begins to play a simple scale progression. With perfect intonation, she ascends and descends, isolating each of my neural cords; and I vibrate gloriously. With his eyes closed, Darío listens to every note I sing, his head nodding a pendulum nod. And I liberate a sound unencumbered by the base desires of those who play me, a clear sound, free from malice.

Scales are pure sound, mathematical progressions of notes. People use scales to make music, to give an aural form to their fears, their aspirations. This human music cannot shake the weight of its creators. There is also the music of animals and natural elements, like the wolf and the wind. But then there is the music of the instruments, the inner vibrations of wooden boxes like myself, of brass cylinders, of tight skin, of metal disks. This is the most silent of all music for only the instruments can hear it. It is the humming that remains when all the notes have been projected, when the instrument is at rest, in peace, dreaming of immortality.

When Madeleine stops playing me, Darío opens his eyes and returns to the harsh reality of not having me in his hands. He despised me earlier, and now he despises himself for wanting to play me again. But he came to Nice for a reason, to dislodge the possibility of Kiara playing me. So, he lets me rest in Madeleine's hands and turns his face away from me.

—You seem to like how it sounds.

—Yes, I do. What about this violin that you don't understand?

—There's so much I don't understand.

—Well, I wasn't too happy with it myself, but you could leave it with me if you want.

—Maybe I should.

*****

With the old port of Nice on her back, Madeleine climbs to the second floor of a red building burnt by the sun. The redness covering the facade defies the fresh blue of the sky. And I wonder why the insolence. She knocks on a door. The pale hands of another woman open the door at once. This other woman, with her pale hands, lays me on a soft divan next to a green parrot inside a white lattice cage. And with those same pale hands, the woman touches Madeleine's face. First her lips, then the line of her jaw. Her hands open the tall window shutters blocking the light. The old port, carrying its boats, its water, and its seagulls, marches into the room. This woman and Madeleine whisper to each other as if keeping secrets. I try to listen, but the words disappear through the window and dive into the waters of the port.

Reclining against a corner of the room, a standing piano waits for something to happen. I guess craving for playing hands to create music. It looks tired, the piano, or maybe bored. Madeleine sits on the bench and plays a few chords, the piano moans with a deep cavernous voice, like a battalion of soldiers marching into the center of the earth. And as if following the march, the woman stands behind Madeleine and places her pale hands on her shoulders. She sways with the music, caressing Madeleine with a gentle touch, moving her hands from the round edge of the shoulders to the base of the neck. And when the music reaches a peaceful *Adagio*, the pale hands turn suddenly and viscously aggressive, and slap the side of Madeleine's head with force. Madeleine keeps on playing, but her tempo decelerates to a very, very slow *Larghissimo*. The pale hands slap her once more on both sides, making her head oscillate like a human metronome.

—Enough, Maria.

—That's my call.

—I don't really know him.

—He played for you. I know he did.

—He wanted to return the violin.

—Nobody else plays for you. I'm the only one who plays for you.

The pale fingers find their way inside Madeleine's mouth, and with a strong tug, make her turn around on the bench. The music dies. Madeleine takes the pale hands within her own hands and begins to kiss them. The pale hands pull away from Madeleine's lips and slap her on the face. Madeleine then kisses the index finger, and the pale hands slap her. She moves on to kissing the middle finger and gets slapped in response. The cycle of tenderness and abuse continues until the ten fingers have been kissed.

I hear the sound of the blows as they land on Madeline's face and feel a tremendous weight on my conscience. I want to burst, crack my body apart. But instead, I sense my strings slackening and my tone slipping away from me. I cannot find notes to denounce the abuse. But I will sing for Madeleine at another time, when it matters most, with my every fiber.

—Why this violin again?

—It sounds eternal.

—What do you know about the eternal?

—Maybe nothing, but I want to play it again.

—You got rid of it once before.

—Maybe that was a mistake.

—Your mistake was to let that man fondle you.

—He didn't touch me.

—He did. With his music he did.

Maria sits down on the bench next to Madeleine. Her pale hands glide over the white and black keys of the piano. The sweetest melody emerges, a soothing melody. Madeleine watches as the abusive hands create this miracle of softness. Her tension melts. And for a moment, the hurt vanishes, leaving behind a field of decapitated daisies. Then Maria changes the melody and starts hammering the keys awfully hard. She plays a punishing staccato, every note growing from the silences in between the two of them, every note harsher, more devastating. And when she reaches an unsustainable crescendo, she slams her pale hands hard on the keyboard, bringing the music to an arresting stop. The sound of a legion of chords crashes against the walls and reverberates inside my wood before emptying itself out the window and onto the port.

—You do as I tell you.

—Maria.

—Don't talk to me now.

—But, Maria...

—Just do as I say. Play Debussy's *Petite Suite, En Bateau.* We'll play it together.

And the four hands begin to move all at once, navigating the keyboard. An apocryphal sound they produce, for the cohesive gentle melody cannot reflect the turmoil of the water underneath—the melodic line serpentines from one end of the keyboard to the other. Their hands sometimes touch, then pull apart. And their torsos oscillate in a facile unison as if the battering had never occurred. Four hands, one music, one lie. Music does not lie, I can attest to that, but the hands that play it do.

At the end of the piece, Madeleine leans over and rests her head on Maria's shoulder. They remain like that, quiet, while the wind from the port enters through the window, circulates around them, and leaves back to the port again credulous of a truce that does not exist. But I do not think like the wind does. This image, endearing, has no permanence, and I will not retain it in my mind. I know about corporal punishment, like the one I just witnessed. I know how the fear lodges into every fiber, wood or flesh, and how it remains latent, like a blind organism at the bottom of the sea, hoping never to see the light of day again. But soon enough the storm will surge, and the waters will part, and the nauseating seaweed will poison you, and the hurt will resurface. The wind will tempest, for it never forgets the impact of her blows. And the hurt will continue until the waters reclaim their stillness. The winds then will flow as if nothing ever happened.

When they finish playing *En Bateau*, Maria kisses Madeleine on her forehead and walks away into a dark hallway that swallows her complete. Madeleine remains at the piano and plays a few loose notes, nothing recognizable, but something close to sadness. The notes do not reach their full sonority; they fall to the ground and crawl a little before lying flat like desiccated anemones. She gives up on the piano and comes to sit next to me on the divan. She stares and I sense her sadness, those depthless eyes revealing a profound disappointment as if all the dismay in the world was traversing through her. And in a fluid motion, Madeleine picks me up and prepares to play me.

I want her to play me. I want her to use me. I want her to purge through me. But she embarks in a display of virtuosity by playing one of Paganini's Caprices. The notes jump and bob around like a butterfly between yellow flowers. Her fingers, dancing on my spine in complete disregard for what broods inside her. This is not possible. I cannot endure the denial. And all at once I tense my body and my neural cords. I hold my breath. And when she digs in for an A sharp on my D string, I twist hard and release a shrieking note that makes Madeleine stop playing at once. She stares at me once again, with disdain this time, and undaunted; she continues to play Paganini. This is how we get hurt, over and over again, when we sing false songs, ignoring our inner voice. This is how she walks on the land with her bare feet while the center of the earth burns in a sordid heat. She now tries to execute a double-stop, but I utter an obtuse sound. She then attempts a pizzicato with her left hand, and I flatten my response. And when she tries to play an array of sixteenth notes ascending from the third position on my E string all the way up to first position on G, I vomit musical mud. I simply claudicate.

She grabs me by the neck and stretches her arm, taking a consummate look at my body. She turns me around. With her knuckles, she knocks my wooden back. She plucks my strings, one at a time, and listens with care. She walks up to the window and takes another look at my body under the reflections the water in the port sends our way. She looks inside my f-holes. She smells the air that exudes from my body. She then walks over to the piano and plays the middle C. With the note fresh in her ears, she bows me, and I sing a pristine C. She lays me back on the divan with utmost care. She sits next to me. With her elbows leaning on her thighs, her face supported by her hands, she whispers.

—I did unto you what was done unto me.

Here, resting on this divan without knowing what would become of me, fearing for my integrity, fearing for Madeleine's sense of herself as a woman, I dream of Kiara. And the dream is not about her hands, but about Kiara as a woman forced to do what she abhors. Kiara indentured, Kiara under the weight of expectations. She, who plays me like a cherub, who plays me not, kept away by Darío, bearing his sex, drinking to forget. Kiara, the agent of my renaissance. I dream of her, but my dream is nothing other than a transparent veil torn by the brutality of the abuse.

Madeleine leaves the room, follows some of the shadows deep into the hallway, and after a few minutes, returns in the company of Maria. Both of them smile, a soft smile, complacent, maybe complicit. They sit next to me on the divan, extending their legs, twisting their arms around each other. I feel the warmth of their bodies. But what I feel with more intensity, is the thickness of their interaction. A person can be next to another and the air between them flow with ease. A person can be next to another, but a sense of doom can make their interaction feel leaden. And lead is what drags this interaction down, Madeleine and Maria's, a silver-colored force that emanates from the continuous abuse and the latent fear. Yes, abuse and fear, the basic elements of jealousy. For what is jealousy but inconsolable fear and a wish to avenge deeds that have yet to happen.

I open my chest and let the air flow into my body. At this moment, my best tactic is to let the world spin around me and wait for the next dramatic upheaval. To pretend that I can alter the results of this interaction is preposterous. I can sing in a variety of ways, even when they play me with martyred resolution, but the ebb and flow of the human-anima is still a mystery to me. So, I lay me down and keep my silence; my right bout touching Madeleine's thigh and my scroll barely rubbing against Maria's abdomen. A bridge between these two elemental forces, a bridge that crashes and burns under the weight of abuse.

—What will you do?

—Play it, what else?

—The bastard isn't even yours.

—I can still play it.

—Will he come back looking for it?

—I don't know, Maria.

—You better find out.

Madeleine leans over me, her body covering my open chest as if protecting me from the potential abuse Maria can unleash. Her breath smells of settled salts or basic settled earth. She then takes me away from the divan and lays me on the piano bench. No, this is not the place for me, especially after the slapping that ensued earlier. But here she leaves me, and, resolutely, she sits next to Maria. In my absence, Maria grows a smile. She kisses Madeleine on the forehead and touches her ears. The two caress each other's faces while their eyes avoid looking my way. And I wonder why they need to distance themselves from me. Why the fear? When in reality, I have no place outside of music, I barely weigh anything, and I sing only when other hands play me. I am virtually nothing.

The sound that emerges from the fusion of Madeleine and Maria reaches and touches me. This is not the sound of punishing hands; this is the sound of hands that sink into flesh and find a river. The sound forms a simple sonata that finds its way into the large belly of the piano where the cords begin to vibrate in gentle unison. And as the unhammered cords absorb the human-made music, they respond in the form of a breath. This breath ascends through the body of the upright piano and spills all over me. I hear how human sounds and the breath of the piano interlace with each other creating a sublime spiral: the source and the echo, the wind and the butterfly.

In this moment, my silence is absolute. I let my senses explore the darkest questions. Can evil and marvel coexist as one? Can a desire to destroy turn into a desire to love within seconds? How are the sounds of human bodies different from the sounds of instruments? Should we use the same notes to write the music of abuse and the music of love? In the same pentagram? Can the notes intermingle with each other as if they originated from the same source as if they elicited the same sensations? How many kinds of music are there? Really, how many kinds of music touch us deep, deeply?

I do not expect any answers. Where would the answers come from? I can only ponder these and so many other questions in the solitude of my mind. I carry on a dialogue with an invisible colloquist who is, at one and the same time, myself and the other, my double. Am I the original or am I the phantasm? This I do not know, but as I lie on this bench,

I come to realize that much is unknown, that much hides from me in the form of sunken memories, that what I see in front of me is only an illusion. Today is Madeleine and Maria; tomorrow is Darío and Kiara. And the same theme repeats itself over and over until all the variations are played to exhaustion. So, I let go of my critical mind. I let go of my musical mind. I simply let go of my sensualist mind. At this moment, I exist only as a wooden box, a mere object of resonance, nothing more. At this moment, I am a lesser violin.

*****

The horn of an elephantine ship penetrates the room announcing that people are about to sail away from the old port. What is so phenomenal about departures? Whoever leaves has to arrive somewhere else. The comings and goings of people are signaled by their sounds. They each have a rhythm and a structure of their own. And they cannot help but announce themselves, a greeting sometimes, a slamming of the door. Sometimes I only hear steps on a wooden floor. They sound the same, whether coming or going, and those are the most difficult sounds to decipher.

A second blow of the horn preludes my own departure. I know I will go somewhere today. Then I hear the sound of slow steps emerging from the hallway, and I prepare for the arrival of Madeleine or Maria, and for ensuing rounds of abuse. But Madeleine arrives by herself, balancing a cup of coffee and looking very tired. She stands in front of me and impales me with her gaze. She places me inside my case and closes the cover. Her steps disappear back into the hallway for a while. When I hear the steps again, they seem to move at a different tempo, much faster this time. The hands that lift me and drag me away are not Madeleine's hands but those of Maria. And off we go down the stairs and into the quay where the intense light and the salty air of the port are happy to devour us.

Maria walks fast. She maneuvers among the crowd of people flooding Place Garibaldi, dodges a few radical mopeds, and avoids getting run over by a cyclist. She miscalculates when turning a corner, and my case crashes against a signpost. My scroll takes the brunt of the blow, but nothing seems to fracture. Maria does not stop. She continues her fast pace through Boulevard Victor Hugo until finally reaching Rue Berlioz. I recognize the street and the shop where they once fixed me. But why does she bring me to the luthier? There is nothing wrong with me. And why does she come alone? I expect the worse.

The old man looks up when she enters the shop and seems pleased to see her. She lays me on the table and opens the case. And upon setting his eyes on me, the old man begins his frenetic routine of pulling down his left earlobe, sneezing, and shaking his head. He tries to keep his composure in front of Maria, but the tics overwhelm him and he runs to the back of the shop to gain some control.

—Just give me a minute, *Mademoiselle.*

—Are you alright?

—Yes, just a minute.

He comes back to the front of the shop looking stiff, making an extraordinary effort to control his body movements. His face is twisted, and his nose all wrinkled. He lifts me up with those brutish yet delicate fingers. He turns me around and looks at my every angle, from my scroll down to my end button, inside my f-holes. He knocks on my back flames; he sniffs me. And with natural delicacy, he lays me down on my case. He turns his back on Maria and does one quick routine of earlobe pulling, sneezing, and head shaking. When he looks at her again, his expression is still and puzzled.

—Yes, *Mademoiselle*, what seems to be wrong with this violin?

—Nothing.

—Exactly!

—There's nothing wrong with it.

—I know.

—But you have seen it before, right?

—Yes, I have. I put a new bridge on it.

—Who brought it to you for repairs?

—Madeleine Toesca. Do you know her?

—Somewhat. But, can you tell where this violin is from?

The luthier's face contorts again. He utters an animal squeal and runs to the back of the store. I hear him squeal a few more times. And there is thumping of his feet on the floor. He may know something I ignore, or maybe he is just a strange man. I wonder. After a minute, he returns with calm composure, as if nothing out of the ordinary has happened. He stands in front of the table facing Maria again and places one hand on top of me. I feel the weight of his massacred fingers pressing me down, and I feel secure.

—*Mademoiselle*, I have no idea where this violin comes from.

—You don't?

—I don't.

—But, do you know about Darío Armand?

—From The Argonauts?

—Yes, The Argonauts.

—Sure… he's been here in the past.

—Did he play this violin?

—He did, and he liked the sound very much.

—Why did he like it so much?

—Because, because…

The luthier bolts away abruptly and runs to the back of the store again. He comes back with a bow I think I recognize. Vuillaume, maybe? He lifts me up and starts to play a few bars of the Spohr's Violin Concerto No. 8 in A minor. And his rude hands caress me, and the pressure of the bow is just correct, and I sing. I sing because I want to sing because he plays me to articulate something, to speak through me. I want him to talk to Maria, to express to her why Madeleine wants to hold on to me, and why Darío wanted to possess me. As a pianist, Maria does not travel with her beloved instrument. She touches the bodies of a legion of mercenaries. But those who play me know me, and ultimately live through me. And she may think of me as her mistress' lover; when in reality, all I do is sing when played by honest fingers. And that may be the cornerstone, the elemental fault. The fingers that play me have an agenda of their own, beyond the beauty music can provide. Those fingers may want a personal glory.

—Can you get in touch with him?

—Darío?

—Yes, that man you call Darío.

—What for?

—Tell him the violin is here waiting for him.

—What about *Mademoiselle* Toesca? Doesn't she want to play this violin?

—Yes, she wants to play this violin, but she's afraid to keep it.

—Afraid… Why?

—Because she's afraid, that's all.

—Sure, I can reach Darío. But what if he's not interested?

—He will be. He can't help it.

Maria does not say anything else. As if nothing mattered, she half closes her eyes, turns around, and steps out of the shop, leaving me in the rough hands of the luthier. The luthier steps up to the door to watch as she walks down Rue Berlioz. He stays at the door until she makes a sharp turn and vanishes out of sight. He entertains his inner thoughts, still looking out into the street. And a few moments later, he comes back to the table where I lie and takes a long look at me. His gaze feels heavy, a sad gaze, maybe the gaze of people who want something they will never get, or maybe the gaze that understands the intrinsic imperfections of the universe.

He lays me inside my case. He closes the case, but before he locks it down, he opens it back up again and watches me in silence for a while. And the heaviness of this gaze makes me uncomfortable. He picks me up. Not bowing my strings, not playing any notes, not emitting a single sound. He only watches as his hands flutter above me like drunken butterflies. But he elicits from me a sweet sound that will never be heard by anyone else other than myself. The beautiful sound of intention when I sing to myself the notes others would love to hear, when I vibrate in a personal way, in unison with the desires of others. To the world, this is a silent sound, but to me, this represents the extension of the perceived universe, the otherness of instruments like myself.

When the interlude is over, the luthier takes care to return me to my case. He tucks me in; he makes sure I am comfortable. This time I do not hang like a bat waiting for a prodigious suitor. This time I can rest and fear nothing. This night traverses its dark space in a silence as miraculous as the black origin of the world. As a nubile mistress, I rest in expectation of what will come. This night I am free to be myself and to imagine what destiny is concocting for me. In this diaphanous moment, I can sing to myself and forget what I have already forgotten, even ignore my unknown origin. Yes, I can exist unencumbered by the load of having to know. This night, the lazy spirits rest and inhale large amounts of air through their mouths, they snore, they sound abysmal. Only creatures of the late night pass me by. A cat, the perfect animal incapable of solfeggio, wants to keep me company.

*****

I wait in silence until the buzz of people brings life to the early morning. The shop absorbs a few clients who come to collect restored instruments. The luthier, looking sharper than yesterday, gets personal with every patron. He connects with them, talks softly in their ears, and plays a soft lullaby when returning their fixed instruments. For the first part of the day, I am as invisible as a useless god. Nobody knows who I am, and nobody seems to care. Even the luthier, who seemed so interested in me when Maria brought me over, has barely looked in my direction. I start to vibrate at a low frequency, more out of boredom than out of fear.

The hours roll smoothly while I practice every iteration of corpse pose. In between breaths, I survey the instruments hanging on the shelf above me and find them very young, green. The smell of their bodies falls over me, a curtain of greenness. Young wood, soft to the music. These bodies have no memory of concerts past. Their fibers have yet to absorb a well-played Bach. I am sure they sing, they certainly do, but without a material memory to guide them. I wonder how they feel when fast fingers play Paganini on their strings. The first time hurts. I wonder how they feel when the music keeps resonating between their ribs. They know more silence than music. They will soon know bad music. Only if they are lucky, will real music come to them. Let them keep their youth for now.

The weight of the late afternoon starts to annoy me. I hear the luthier shaving wood in the backroom but cannot tell if he is creating or repairing. That is where the magic happens, in the backroom. Here, in the front, it is only vanity. If this day is one of many days to come, death has knocked at my door. I have rested before. I may have slept for centuries. But the idea of resting in limbo, just when a master like Amédée wrote an original piece of music for me, is insufferable.

I hear metal now, tools, a saw. I hear the voice of a Cremonese coming out of the little square box, inspired, singing the beloved Spohr. I hear the voice of the luthier in conversation with nobody.

—*Monsieur* Armand?

—

—It's the luthier, in Nice.

—

—Very well, thank you. Remember that violin?

—

—Well, I have it in my shop again.

—

—No, she didn't. Her friend did.

—

—Nothing wrong.

—

—I thought you wanted to have it.

—

—Is that right?

—

—No, nobody.

—

—Yes, until 7pm. I have my dinner late.

—

—Perfect.

*****

This new morning is bearable just because of its potential. The afternoon, however, is quick to offer nothing but the validation that the day is half-dead. And lying here, collecting dust, becomes more of a drag in this insipid afternoon when I expect Darío to show up any minute but does not show up at all. Today the shop is desolate. Where are the numerous patrons inquiring about their instruments like they did yesterday? How about a discussion about a wolf tone? No, nothing of the sort. All I hear are recorded concerts by popular heroes, the recognized gods regurgitating performances for the accepting ears. This is how music is destroyed; when expectations are created by the devilish craft of reproduction, killing spontaneity and the very soul of the instrument. How can an instrument sing freely if its very song needs to emulate the voice of an accepted hero? Legion instruments die when only a few are considered holy, the rest, lesser creatures worthy of tomb silence. I have entertained these thoughts before, but now they come to the forefront because I am deep in the stupor of this boring shop.

And my train of thought gets derailed by the entrance of the very Darío of my memories who walks past me and heads for the back of the shop. The luthier must be surprised by his sudden appearance. They spoke yesterday, but I doubt the luthier believed Darío would actually return to Nice so soon. They say a few words to each other, mainly pleasantries, and without hesitation the luthier comes to the front of the shop and brings Darío to where I am lying in my recumbent position, exposing my belly to the world, vulnerable.

Darío takes a good look at me. He leans forward and reaches for my bouts but stops halfway. He backs off and clasps his hands behind his back. Like a scolded child, he waits for the luthier to give him permission to grab me. The luthier says nothing and makes no gestures. Darío then grabs me, and I feel the pressure of his fingers all over my body. His disgusting touch makes me want to screech. But I do not. Instead, I think of another time and another place, of the soft hands of Kiara, of the sound of a Bach partita. In time, he will bring me close to Kiara. He cannot help it. So, I tolerate him handling me at will.

The luthier brings a bow from the back of the shop and asks Darío to tune me. I am not out of tune. I know that. But when Darío plays my open A string, I twist my body slightly and shift the pitch higher. He turns my peg ever so slightly and plays my open A again. Now I relax my body and shift down the pitch. He does not like the sound. He compares it with my open E string which sounds perfectly fine. He tries turning my peg again and plays me to confirm the result. I do not sound well because I do not want to sound well. He repeats the process, but each time I twist my body shifting up and down, denying him the right tone. He asks the luthier for another bow but the luthier says there is nothing wrong with the one he is using. Darío knows there is nothing wrong with the bow but he insists. The luthier brings him another bow and Darío tries to make my A string sound as it should. That is what he wants, but that is not what I want. After a few more attempts, he stops trying to right what is not wrong and lays me down on the table. He steps back, his jaw hanging, his arms hanging, his sense of mastery shattered.

—Just like before!

—What do you mean?

—I play the right notes, but the violin sounds out of tune.

—Are you sure it's the violin?

—Are you implying I don't know how to play?

—I think it's got a beautiful sound.

—So, I'm the one with the problem then.

—No, I don't mean that.

—What do you really mean?

—I mean that the violin sounds great some times. Other times, it just doesn't sound right.

—That's what I said.

—Yes, but you blame yourself.

—No, I blame the violin.

—But the violin doesn't have a mind of its own. It cannot change the way it sounds.

—So, you're blaming me for the bad sound.

—I'm not blaming you for anything. I'm saying the violin has no will.

—Do you think I'm an idiot?

The luthier, bothered by the harshness of the exchange,

contorts his face and launches into an episode of pulling down his left earlobe, sneezing, and shaking his head before responding to Darío.

—*Monsieur*, I would never say such a thing.

—I don't think you would, but it sounds as if you're saying just that.

—*Je suis désolé.*

—No need to apologize. Let me try to play something.

Darío lets the full weight of his chin bear on me. He seems intent on dictating. His gaze runs up and down my body, his left hand grabs on to my spine. He does not squeeze, but he holds me tightly. I feel his muscles contracting, transmitting the tension onto me. And the tighter he gets, the lesser the chance to produce a beautiful sound. Even if I were to cooperate with him, his brutish approach is certain to kill the sublime. I relax and allow my strings to vibrate freely. Without any tempering on my end, I could sound like the very wooden box that I am. But how should my natural wood vibrate under pressure? And if I were to take time into consideration, how could I forget the memory of former sounds? How could I pretend that no other sounds ever traversed my body? This, I think, as he plays Paganini's Caprice No. 24 in A minor, the sliding, the double-stops, the pizzicato. He plays me hard. He takes possession of my body.

I let the sound escape through my f-holes but take no pride on the end result. I simply allow my body to resonate, without my personal imprint, without the minuscule movements of my ribs. I sound as uninspired as a lesser violin in a forsaken orchestra. And this is the sound his abusive grip generates. This is the sound he will get today. Darío, with the capacity to extract the most out of my body, will genuflect to mediocrity, for I will not push myself any further. He lays me down on the table and looks up at the luthier as if he were responsible for the disappointment. The luthier, not knowing how to deal with the monster in front of him, simply caresses my body as if he were caressing the body of a wounded soldier.

—Darío, that's enough.

—What's enough?

—You don't need to play anymore.

—Because I won't get anywhere with this?

—No, because the two of you aren't communicating.

—What can this violin tell me?

—The violin already told you. You're the one not responding.

—Are you crazy?

—No, no, no… You don't understand. I'm a luthier. I talk to violins all day.

—So, what has this violin told you?

—You don't want to know.

With his rude hands, with his apparent indifference, the luthier has been listening to me attentively. He must know everything about Madeleine, and he must also know what Maria is capable of doing. Clearly, he knows about Darío and his frustration with me. I wonder what else he knows. Does he know about Kiara and the way I feel about her, about her hands? Does he know about Venice, not the Venice he can see with his own eyes, but the Venice of before, the one I have a hard time remembering? Does he know where I come from? The origin of my wood? Does he know why I sound the way I sound? I wonder if he knows about my fears. To what extent does he know my deficits, my flaws? And even more wicked, does he know things about me that I have yet to figure out?

Darío gets out of the shop and lights a cigarette in the plenitude of the street. I hate when he smokes and plays me right away. I hope he will not come back into the shop to play another piece. He seems to be talking to himself, the hands gesticulating, the lips flapping, and nobody next to him. He finishes that cigarette and lights a second one. The luthier goes to the back of the shop and abandons me here, on top of the table, completely exposed. Alone, between these two opposing minds, I rest on the table and imagine an open G, deep, clear, earth promising.

No real time can pass as slow as the time in waiting. In music, notes are accountable to time, and the silences are accountable as well. Everything moves forward at a pre-scribed tempo. Maestros may disagree about the relationship between *allegro* and real time, but in the end, a relationship exists. In waiting, a minute could be a year, and its tempo could be *agitato*, rarely *gioioso*, and most likely *mesto*. And as I wait here, I wish for time to stop being time and hope for other hands to lift me. I wait, and nothing happens. I wait some more. I enter a *caesura* with no beginning or end, where time is no longer counted. "Sing, o goddess, the rage…" time, time, time, time, a long time, a short time… "of Achilles, the son of Peleus." But I am not the son or the daughter of any man, woman, or instrument. And if I were, I have no knowl-edge of their identities, singular or plural.

The door opens and Darío storms into the shop talking to himself as if convincing his spirit of an irrevocable truth. He approaches me and spills over an intensity I have not seen before. He calls the luthier and demands that I be placed in my case and handed over to him at once. The luthier proceeds to lift me from the table and places me inside my case. He does not close the cover. Instead, he brings me to the back of his shop, clears his workbench, and lays me down with care. Darío follows him and once again demands to take me away immediately. The luthier ignores the urgent demands and focuses his attention on me. With his rude fingers, he touches my belly, my strings. He taps my bridge three times. And then he leans over and whispers into my f-holes: "Hieronimo Venier." I will always remember that name.

—*Monsieur* Darío, the violin is yours to take home.

—I'm not going home.

—Where are you going?

—Back to Barcelona, my colleagues are waiting for me.

—The Argonauts?

—Yes, we have a new composition to master.

—Do you think you can master anything with this violin?

—I will, even if it kills me.

—Don't kill the violin. Even if it kills you.

The blue of the Mediterranean extends far, and it cannot be mistaken for any other blue. This blue tone plays at the bottom of my memories. I cannot recall when I saw it for the first time, but I know I found it different from the North Adriatic, my first sea. The tranquility, the sea of tranquility is an alluring passage. I like to be swallowed by that emotion but not by its waters. And this time I follow the sea while resting on Darío's lap. Like a seagull, I open my wings to the blue and let the words of the luthier flutter inside my body.

THE GHOSTS

Sometimes I need soothing. But even when all the melodies contribute their best, the collective balm fails me and I find not a note, nor a phrase, capable of settling me. I cannot even sing a rotten lullaby. Maybe my body has stiffened and my strings hardened as iron shafts. But I know this cannot true. The sense of helplessness is not corporeal; it is not bound to my body, but to my weariness. Perhaps re-entering the world of The Argonauts brings about this nasty sense of emptiness. But I also come back into the potential of Kiara's hands. This may trigger a completely different weariness. The weariness of uncertainty.

I contemplate the old walls and the people moving about in their external habitats. This external life makes it more difficult to bestow abuse on anyone because the passersby are watching. Physical abuse that is, for the psychological kind flourishes no matter exposure or visibility. That is what hurtful words can do; they get under your skin where they live invisible lives, where the sun cannot penetrate. But abuse in the form of words is not the only one that hides. Silence, when used as punishment, also achieves invisibility. Nobody would ever hear when you are not spoken to. The castigating extrusion of commentary, of validation, agreement or disagreement, creates a void as abusive as any blow-by-word or fist.

I think these thoughts because Barcelona receives me with open arms. As for The Argonauts, I wonder if they will consider my arrival in the same light. Darío is the bearer of my body, conflicted, even despised by the rest of them. The fact that he brings me back could already predispose an antipathy. Not from Kiara; I hope not, but perhaps from Leon. He is changeable like an anemone floating in tempestuous waters. Nobody can tell what he would do when he does not get his fix, or when he gets more of a fix than he needs. Angelo is essentially benign; so, I should not fear him. But maybe I think these thoughts because I doubt my own wishes. Do I want to rejoin them, The Argonauts? An interesting thought, for I wonder if my will extends beyond the realm of sound. Do I really have a will? My will, an entity made out of nothing, not of wood or metal, nor of sound. What is will then? A current, a nervous tick, a tendency? Or is it the juice that drips out of obstinate convictions? I better let go of this melody before it sours my spirit.

Darío enters the *Ciutat Vella* with a sense of belonging. He moves through the tight alleys with confidence, pretending he knows how to step on this shifting ground. He heads straight for the *Palau de la Música,* and I sense he has scheduled a rehearsal with the rest of The Argonauts, or a meeting with Amédée, or both. Once at the *Palau,* he finds a small and quiet rehearsal room on the first floor, he lays me on the floor and sits on a chair looking up to the ceiling. He sits there in silence. I know this must be hell for him, for I never saw him meditate before. Maybe he needs to reassert his position among The Argonauts. He introduced me to the quartet and then he let me go as if I were his demise. He complained about me. At times he played me when he must have sensed I was playing him. And, somehow, Amédée recognized I have a unique voice. And he wrote this piece, an immaculate piece to this day. The truth is that Darío may be the weakest of all. He wavers when others hold still.

The first one to come into the room is Leon. He drags his

cello as if it were a dead body. Maybe that is how it feels to him, a beefy musical box that needs to be buried. His taciturn eyes scan the room, they pause briefly over Darío, then over me, before he squanders his visual faculties on a bouquet of dead flowers. He opens the case and brings out his cello. With its wide hips, the cello struggles to stand straight, but Leon grabs its waist and long spine and forces it to be upright, in the middle of the room, with a modicum of grace. Nothing hurts more than to watch another instrument assume an imposed role without putting up a fight. But maybe the cello has learned to accept, to endure, to live for the music and not for the hands.

But what do I live for? For the music? I want to believe I do. Do I live for the hands that play me? Well, I often dream of Kiara's hands, and in those dreams, there is no music, only silence. Do I live for the discovery of my origin? A complicated proposition that is. Perhaps I live because I have no other choice. That would be a sad reality. Or perhaps I live because I have yet to sing my most beautiful song. As ridiculous as that sounds, there may be some truth in that romantic idea. Maybe I just live because I am an instrument, instrumental in the nebulous realities of those who play me. That would place me in a subordinate position; that is how I get hurt.

The room brightens when Amédée enters and greets Darío with enthusiasm. He shakes Leon's hand and immediately turns towards me. I feel his gaze traversing my body. Leon says something and so does Darío, but the intensity of Amédée's gaze blurs all sounds in the room, and their words dematerialize. He grabs me with his left hand and supports my spine without pressing hard on me. He holds me there, not playing my strings, just listening to my breath. I relax every fiber in my body and vibrate at my natural wooden rate. My body as spruce, maple, and ebony.

—You brought it back, Darío.

—Yes, but I wonder if that was a good idea.

—But you went back to Nice to fetch for it.

—I did. But I don't know exactly why.

—Well, I'm happy you did. The whole piece depends on its sound.

—But who can get the sound out of it?

—Haven't we spoken about this before?

—I may not be capable. Maybe I don't want to play anything.

—Don't play "anything," play something marvelous instead.

Amédée may have knowledge beyond what he reveals. He speaks as if he understands Darío and his limitations. I wonder if he knows what my origin is. Why would he write a whole composition based on my potential sound, let alone Darío's capacity to elicit that sound?

Amédée lays me on top of a chair and steps away, leaving the rehearsal room where a deep silence grows. Neither Darío nor Leon say a word. They fumble through the music sheets as if there was something important there. Nothing really, only the music they have played multiple times. After a few awkward minutes, Kiara enters the room and says hello to the two of them. The greeting goes unanswered. She says hello again, and Darío mutters a weak response I cannot decipher. She sets her violin on the chair next to mine and quickly walks out of the rehearsal room. I want to go after her and beg her to play me. But I want so many things that will never take place. So, I lie on my back and try to ignore the sight of Darío and Leon pretending to be at ease. I take comfort in the mystery of Amédée's knowledge and let the minutes roll down the walls, around the legs of the chair supporting me, and out the door into the old streets.

What is the destiny of a wooden box? Do I understand the world differently because of my wood? Would I look at eternity in a different way if my ribs were covered by flesh? Soft, sweating, oozing, glandular flesh? Truly, if I were made of flesh, would I be able to endure through the centuries as a living, singing being? Why do I feel the immediacy of human yearning when my nature is more permanent? Is it really more permanent? Is it really... anything?

When the doors open up again at 3:30 pm, Kiara and Angelo walk inside and take their places in the rehearsal room. Without pomp or circumstance, without any words, The Argonauts prepare for what will likely be a momentous rehearsal. They all lift their instruments and look at each other to confirm their readiness. The music sheets rest on the stands, but nobody is looking at them. And after a quick nod from Darío, a harmonious phrase enters in D minor.

Nothing but the universe, nothing but the accumulated yearning spreading in the form of sound, nothing but a mental construct of what eternity would be if written for the pentagram. Nothing, or everything, or nothing at all. The sound gathers its own gut; it pushes with a strong shoulder, it spreads its arms in front as if swimming under water. The sound has a life of its own, independent of the four instruments; it lives untainted by the neurotic exchanges among The Argonauts. The sound owes itself to The Argonauts, yes it does, but at the same time, it lives as if life were bestowed on it, no strings attached. It draws blood from the communal vein of The Argonauts, but it does not bleed for them. The sound, the composition Amédée created based on my capacity, flutters in the air.

When the first movement is over, nobody asks for a break. The faces of The Argonauts burn like a morning in August. They look at each other, they nod. At once they catapult themselves into the second movement, and I feel the need to shine. I know I can shine in a moment like this, when the hands that play me want to elicit the best sound possible, not for the audience, but for themselves. These are the moments I live for, the private miracles when things happen because they deserve to happen. And without a clear agenda, without understanding the complete implications of our virtuosity, The Argonauts rehearse Amédée's piece and make it sound divine. And I realize I exist, even if only for this instant.

All the hands come to rest while the music still travels far beyond the room, the notes gaining distance from each other as they ascend toward the Barcelona sky. My wooden fibers tremble, the air inside my belly expands and contracts. The Argonauts seem paralyzed, not saying a word, not moving from their chairs. What just happened was not witnessed by anyone but ourselves. Did we sound as marvelous as I think, or is this only my imagination? Am I projecting my grandiose wishes, a mythical concept of myself? I am not sure, but the unreal expression on Darío's face tells me that something extraordinary just happened. And Leon is crying, sobbing. Kiara leans over and caresses my back with her long fingers. My maple flames erupt.

A secret miracle. I may have seen one before when I sang Giambattista's composition. But this, if it really happened, is finer, unexpected, accidental, impossible. But who played whom? Did Darío make me sing at my utmost or did I make him play at his best? I am sure he is as surprised as I am, for he could not have expected such harmony between us. Are we not capable of influencing each other? And if none of us expects the other to achieve greatness, does greatness happen only by chance? If greatness is unachievable, there would be no point in rehearsing. Maybe great performances exist inside people's heads, completely detached from the reality of the music being played.

I try to recapitulate the music we just played, but the phrases evade me. I know we played three movements but cannot tell how long they were. The key was D minor, that much I can recall. But what was the piece all about? I try to figure it out, but not a single passage comes to my mind. I look for clues on Kiara's face, on Angelo's face, but they seem transfixed, unable to tell a story. And Leon, he weeps. The space inside the rehearsal room starts to feel small and claustrophobic. From the expansive greatness to the diminishing actuality of our quartet inside a room of four walls. And as I start to feel the weight of reality, the door opens, and Amédée walks in like a comet in the dark.

—I just heard the most wonderful composition. Whose piece was that?

—Amédée, we just finished playing your piece.

—Yes, Darío, I heard my piece. And you did a phenomenal job. But the one you played after mine. That was beautiful and so intriguing.

—We just played your piece.

—And I thank you for finally making it sound as I had intended. That makes me very, very happy. But I'm still curious about the other piece.

—You could ask Kiara or Angelo. We only played your composition.

—Well, I'm not so sure.

—What do you mean Kiara?

—I mean that I'm not so sure we only played Amédée's work.

—But what else could we have played? Look at your sheet music. It's right there.

—You're right Darío, there's only Amédée's composition. But I also think I heard something else.

—But what else is there to hear? We've been playing these three movements for the last 30 minutes. Are you hallucinating?

—We've been playing for close to an hour.

—No, that's not true.

—Look at the clock, 4:30 pm.

—Angelo, Angelo?

—I don't really know.

—Leon?

—Don't bother with Leon. I think he's sick again.

—I'm not sick. I played something great, but I've got no idea what it was.

—You're sick.

—Darío, please. Stop it.

—He can take it. He can take needles.

—Leave him alone.

—Can you do it again? Can you conjure that mysterious music once more?

—What's there to do Amédée? Get confused and play the wrong music again?

—You played my music perfectly, but then you played something even better.

—Enough of this bullshit! I'm leaving. And you three can figure out what you think you were playing. Write it down too, while you're at it.

He leaves the rehearsal room, Darío, in anger and confusion. He does not even bother to take me with him. I am sure he did not want to find himself in this predicament, in front of Amédée. This is clearly not about me but about his own doubts. He takes everything so personally, even the things that have no clear connection to anybody like the birth of music out of thin air. Nobody should be blamed for that. I always felt that not every note I sing is written on the pentagram. Why fight it? What difference does it make if I serve as a conduit of inevitable music? The universe has a need to speak. So many voices need to be heard, and so many have no instrument to bring them forth. Why the silences when not everything has been said? Why the repetition when unique voices are awaiting? Hands play me, and I sing the written songs. I admit my shortcomings. But if the moment comes when music writes itself, out of need or desperation, out of a yearning for beauty, or simply out of nothingness; I am ready to open my body and let that music traverse me.

*****

And once again, left behind by Darío, a man who cannot grasp the needs of the universe, I find myself in Kiara's hands. This unrequested tenderness makes me feel I belong to her, partially. I long to be with her, but this only happens by chance. And once with her, other hands claim me, and I end up hurt. I would like a different kind of transition. From loving hand to loving hand, or even better, from loving hand to no other hand; a reality that evades me. So, I naturally wonder what awful things will happen to me next.

Her hands take me away from the rehearsal room, through streets that have no meaning to me, to a little café in *Barrio de Gràcia*, where she places me on the floor next to her violin and orders a glass of cava. She seems happy to be here, away from the pressure that Darío imparts on her, taking the air as it comes, and letting the universe exist. She drinks her cava and looks at us, her instruments. I like to think she considers me as hers as much as she does this other one. To my surprise, she opens my case and takes me out in the middle of the plaza. She adjusts the shoulder rest to match the length of her neck. And when she feels comfortable, she plays a few notes, nothing extraordinary, just a simple mazurka. She lets the notes drip in the most natural way. And the simple song fills the plaza where people listen and accept the music as a gift. There is beauty in simplicity, and this is proof. When people go about their business in syntony with the music surrounding them, they participate in the creation of musical normalcy. And each generation and place carves a normalcy of its own.

Kiara continues to play a variety of popular Spanish songs. She does not ask for money; she does not ask for anything. She may be evaluating how I sound in the relaxed setting of this plaza in the late afternoon. She must be curious about my raw sound. The way I sound away from concert halls. Then, a little boy lets go of his mother's hand and runs toward Kiara with a red rose in his hands. He stops right in front of us. Kiara continues to play me softly. The boy leaves the rose on the ground and runs back to hide behind his mother's skirt. From there, he keeps looking our way. Kiara holds me steady and takes the rose with her right hand. She smells the fragrance. She tries to make eye contact with the boy, but he is now completely invisible behind his mother. After tucking the rose behind her ear, Kiara begins to play the most tender berceuse. The boy peeks from behind his mother's skirt, making sure not to expose any part of his body. When Kiara finished the piece, he dashes diagonally across the plaza in the direction opposite from us, and his mother follows after him calling his name.

Kiara places me on the chair next to her and orders another glass of cava. She stares at me. I wonder what she sees in me. She drinks half of the glass all at once and continues to study my body. As I take on her gaze, I begin to feel as if she is playing me. The simple harmonic motion of my wooden fibers increases in amplitude and I ring in C sharp. Inaudible at first, but as the music continues to reverberate inside my body, it spills out, and I exude. I hum. The notes do not respect any tempo. My inner music plays light and unencumbered. And I feel as if time surpasses time, gliding away from itself. Everyday contains a moment when I think I will touch immortality. And this is my moment for as long as this moment lasts.

When I manage to focus on Kiara again, she has already finished her glass of cava and leans back on her chair with her eyes closed. Her expression, a field of wind-sung grass, tells me she has touched some of that immortality. Or at least, she has seen its silhouette. We remain in silence and watch as people start to congregate in the plaza. The empty chairs get occupied. The sound of a multitude of voices infiltrates every corner of the plaza, and the buzz of life begins to boil. A solitary woman sits at the table next to ours and asks for a *caña*.

She takes a cigarette from a mushed-up package and places it between her fingers. She does not light the cigarette, but she still brings it to her lips. A habit, perhaps, or a consoling strategy. She seems distracted, or maybe she is daydreaming. I cannot tell. After scanning the entire plaza, she turns to our table and waits for Kiara to pay attention to her.

—What a lovely violin!

—Yes, lovingly lovely.

—Will you play some later?

—Oh no… I don't know how to play.

—Is that right? So what are you doing here?

—Who? The violin or me?

—Both, I suppose.

—Well… I'm here to listen to the violin.

—But who will be the one playing it?

—Nobody needs to play it. It plays itself.

—Oh well… I've never heard of such a thing.

—Neither had I.

*****

The narrow stairs are slanted, all the way to the fifth floor, and the incompetent lights make climbing a disorienting experience. We enter Kiara's rental flat where a vase hugs dried white flowers on a center table. Beyond the table, there is a small window overlooking the plaza where we just touched immortality. This is her vantage point. This is how she looks upon the world. She uses perspective and distance to deal with Darío, and the same approach allows her to play me with sensitive hands. She is inside the world but at the same time outside of it. She can dance in the rain, she can play music within four walls, and she can descend to the underworld to play jazz. She can even make love to Darío when possessed by alcohol. And she can let me sound as an unbridled musical box. Limitless, she is.

I listen carefully, hoping to catch a musical phrase stock under the eaves of the building, or twirling around a chimney. But nothing of what we played in the plaza remains. All the notes have already ascended to the atmosphere and must be joining with the sounds of the day. Because all the sounds, once their time is past, enter a vast amalgam of vibrations that merges and travels to the stars. Other sounds get absorbed by material bodies in close proximity, like people, animals, plants, concrete, and dirt. These bodies vibrate in turn and produce their own sounds that will travel to the stars as well. Every audible entity rises to the stratosphere and loses itself in the process.

Kiara moves around the small apartment in a sort of frenzy, and I wonder what makes her anxious. She may not be anxious at all, but the moving around seems more than necessary. She relegates her own violin to a dark corner of the room where it cannot see life unfolding down in the plaza. She takes me in her hands, sits at a chair next to the window, and touches my neural cords with her fine hands. She does not play me; she only caresses me. I let go of my expectations and let the air from the plaza filter through my f-holes. I simply let my body absorb the touch. I stay quiet; I make no sounds. And this is when I know I truly exist, because all the fibers in my body, whether they are maple, spruce, mahogany, steel, or dried varnish, are aware and responsive. I feel like a real violin, even if I am a lesser one.

The sun layers a coat of red and yellow on the buildings

across the plaza. I try to think of nothing. I try not to assign musical notes to a physical experience. But Kiara's way persuades me to weave through the millions of notes I have sung in the past and entices me to find patterns and associations that can explain the afternoon sun. I pause and try to vacate my mind. But her touch, her humming, and the voluminous colors dominate me. I start to purr an ode to the moment, to my being here.

A punctuated pizzicato at the door interrupts the composition. All eyes and ears focus on the wooden door that swings open, revealing the impertinent entrance of the little devil. Of all the devils in the world, it is our little devil. He, with his beardless face, comes into the flat and stands in the middle of the room to observe how Kiara touches me. I stop making any sounds, or music, or guttural noises that could be construed as music. I turn into a silent box. He, the little devil, smiles an ample smile as if his presence were a gift. I respond by tightening my every fiber and tensing my cords. Kiara senses my reactions and places her palm on my flamed back. I cannot understand why the little devil finds his way into my reality at this importunate moment. He took me places I had not seen before, I must admit, but right now I want to be here on my own terms, in the sole presence of Kiara. But my thoughts remain my thoughts, and neither Kiara, nor the little devil, truly understand the way I think or feel. This, a detriment to my existence, for I need them to open the world for me, to protect me, to bring me to where I can shine. And the thought of them as a couple disturbs me, even if I understand that they must be a couple. What else, why not?

The little devil advances. He enters deep into the room,

and I feel a slight tremor in Kiara's hand. This can be fear, but at the same time, it can be desire. She stops humming, and I fall into an abyss, an absence. And the closer the little devil gets, the less I matter to Kiara. And I know this is true because the pressure of her hands on my body has weakened. She barely holds on to me. I fear she will drop me on the floor.

Once in front of Kiara, the little devil focuses his attention exclusively on me. He grabs me away from her and tucks me under his chin. Kiara does not resist; to the contrary, she seems content to let me go. She does not abandon me, but she gives me as a bequest. And the little devil starts to move around the room while playing loose notes. He does not follow any predetermined musical arrangement. He simply plays polyrhythms and syncopations derived from his own mind. He emphasizes speed and dissonance, and I feel like I am in that basement once again—the Korsakof.

Kiara's eyes follow him, follow me. She remains in the center of the room while the little devil makes me sing odd tunes. I enjoy the stretch, the challenge. I feel my body pulled from different angles. I meet the uncertainty of notes in-between notes, and nothing follows the expected. At this point, I could be the song, or the instrument, or the very player. We merge, the little devil and I, and that liberates me while at the same time, it frightens me to the core.

—Sweet, real sweet my old fiddle friend.

—I just got it from Darío. He actually left it behind at the *Palau.*

—What's the story with him?

—Who, Darío or the violin?

—Both.

—Darío will get Amédée's endorsement. I know he will. We played his entire composition today. Bold and lyrical— truly extraordinary. But something incredible happened there.

—What happened?

—I don't know yet.

—But what happened?

—We played as if time didn't exist.

—For how long did you play?

—I'm not so sure.

—You don't know?

—I'm not so sure. And then the violin…

—This violin?

—Yes, it sounded like never before. And I don't think it was Darío who made it sound that way.

—What are you talking about?

—I really don't know.

But what is there to know? How can we be certain about a live performance? The miracle occurred and ended, and nothing remains but the confused memory of having heard something extraordinary. Or, perhaps, having heard something not worth remembering. And even if we remember a particular performance, how do we manage to compare it with another one? Are we to trust our memories, are we to validate them when everything tosses and turns inside our minds, and what we believe happened is only a figment of our distorted imagination? Can we compare an impossibility with another one? I have serious doubts. I even have a hard time remembering how I sung in the times before this time. When I try to recall how I sounded inside those palaces at the edge of the Grand Canal, when inspired fingers played me, all I recover is the sound of murky water splashing against old stones. But Kiara seems to believe I sounded differently, and her assertion touches me, deeply.

With his beardless chin, the little devil taunts the world outside the window. He points his chin straight to the center of the plaza, egging the water in the fountain to jump. The notes jump, syncopated, and so does Kiara's heart while she sees me in his hands, singing notes of nothingness. He defies the cannon, the little devil; he deviates from anything written by anyone before. Yes, he is challenging the musical possibilities of the moment. But what happened earlier today challenged the accumulated musical expectations and time itself.

—So you don't know.

—I felt it, but I don't know what it was.

—Was it different from jazz?

—Yes, completely different. It happened. But when it happened and how it happened escapes me.

—And how's that possible?

—That's what I don't know.

—Can you replicate that sound?

—I don't want to replicate anything.

—But why not?

—It's not my sound; it doesn't belong to me. It seems to exist on its own.

Yes, I do exist on my own, but that very existence is a murky one. Can I claim every note I sing as my own? Probably not. My voice is mine, mostly. But when my voice speaks apocryphal tones, I feel usurped, raped, and abused. Synchronicity exists between the outer confines of my voice and my very core. That is when miracles happen.

Kiara grabs the little devil's chin and gracefully takes me away from his hands. She walks towards the window and pauses to absorb the mischievous light bouncing from wall-to-wall, tantalizing the water fountain. She grabs me by the scroll, stretches her arm, and holds me outside the window where I hang exposed to the winds that flood the plaza. And as I hang over the expanse, I hear the children and their dogs, the women and their yearnings, the men and their cigarettes, the roar of the trafficking bodies. I feel like I am about to choke on the cacophony of a world outside my world. I take a deep breath. I abandon my fears. I let the air flow through me, and I hum.

She holds me, Kiara, without constraining me, allowing me to exude my response to the world. And the composition resembles nothing known to me, an inner voice, a voice of my own that I have never heard. The little devil approaches the window and watches. He tries to reach out to grab me, but Kiara slaps his hand hard. A hard slap. She does not say a word to him for she is listening to my hum, absorbed as I am in this space outside music. I think I resonate in D minor, or perhaps F major. I could be singing in both scales or neither. I could be mute and not know it. I could be simply hanging here while the real music is happening in the plaza below me.

Down in the plaza, a man with a bottle of beer in his hand walks toward the window and stops to look up at me as I hang from Kiara's hands. He takes a long drink from the bottle and looks up again as if wondering something. He takes another drink and starts talking.

—Drop it. Drop it now! I'm here to take it home.

Kiara does not respond; she keeps holding me while ignoring the man.

—Go ahead, darling. Let it go!

—There's no letting go.

—Then why are you dangling the thing?

—Can you hear it?

—What, the mopeds?

—No, the violin.

—Oh honey, I hear nothing.

—What about the music?

—Let go, let go. Just drop it.

The man in the plaza does not hear the music. Kiara hears some aspects of the music. I hear all the music my body projects. And the little devil pretends to hear everything but, in reality, only absorbs minimally. And maybe this discrepancy comes from the divergent nature of ourselves. How could we all hear the same music when each of us responds according to our individual predisposition, nature, or willingness? I play music that belongs to each musical period known to man, but I also play music that belongs to no time. I may play music that travels submerged, in the depths of my unconscious. Perhaps that is the universal music which we all share collectively.

Kiara does not drop me; instead, she tightens her grip around my scroll and pulls me inside the room. She grabs the bunch of white dried flowers from the vase and throws them out the window. The man in the plaza thanks her with a loud screech. She stands in front of the little devil with her back to the open window holding me really tight. She does not move, and she does not let go of me.

—Where did you really find this violin?

—I told you, the old man on 54th Street sold it to me. I really didn't pay much for it.

—But where is it from? Did he say anything about Venice?

—He didn't know, the old man, and he didn't seem to care either. He wanted to sell me something expensive. You know his kind.

—Something doesn't make sense. Darío wants it some days, and then he wants to get rid of it. There are moments it sounds like an angel, and then it croaks like a toad. And then it seems to mediate between our souls and the rest of the universe.

—What do you mean?

—It transcends.

—What does it transcend?

—All of us, you and I, and Darío. It plays beyond the music. And its body expands to the confines of the universe.

—Easy, Kiara. This is a cheap violin.

—But you've played it. And you've heard me play it.

—Maybe the magic is in your hands.

—No, I've got no magic, even if I want to believe I do. This is about the violin.

—Or, you and the violin. The two of you. That's where the magic is.

The little devil reaches to touch Kiara's face. This time she slaps his hand even harder.

—Don't insult me.

—I just want to touch you.

—Don't touch me.

She turns away from him and goes back to the window. After contemplating the plaza with the multitude of people and sounds, she pulls me close to her bosom, and her embrace engulfs all of me. Without her bow, without any intentions to play me, Kiara closes her eyes and lets the air swirl around us. And then she speaks loudly for the little devil to hear.

—When I turn around, I trust that you will no longer be here.

*****

Only discord can be expected when The Argonauts come together outside the rehearsal room. And I am not disappointed when I find myself in the tight space of Darío's rented flat, where The Argonauts battle each other, and nobody seems the victor. They lunge at each other with sharp words while I remain quiet. Their dissonant opinions create a perfect disharmony. Kiara sits next to me and touches my body. And for an instant, I fall into a deep blue sea.

—And what do you propose Leon?

—I propose nothing. That's what I propose.

—Oh, Leon, not so easy my friend.

—Listen… I already told you. Your playing is erratic. We never know what we're going to hear from you.

—Didn't I sound magnificent in the rehearsal?

—The violin did.

—That's not fair.

—Kiara said the same thing, ask her.

—You played very well, and the violin sounded like nothing I've heard before.

—That's my point! The violin sounded great, but not because he played it.

—You're so smart, Leon. Does the violin play itself?

—No, it doesn't, but you were not the one who made it sound that way.

—This is ridiculous. We all played our best.

—You did, Angelo, but I don't know about him.

—Enough! Amédée wrote this piece for this one violin, but the ensemble has to excel.

—So, are you going to keep the violin this time or are you going to sell it, or forget it, or something?

—I didn't mean to leave it behind.

—Well, you did.

—No, he didn't. I decided to take the violin with me.

—Kiara, Kiara.

That which she touches blooms. Kiara's hands and words bring about a certain beauty that disarms. The Argonauts know that she is lying. She did not decide to take me with her *a priory*. She decided to rescue me, and in the process, rescue them. Perhaps she decided to explore the music beyond the music, to extend her hands and touch the humming of the world. I cannot be certain, but her sensitivity makes me believe she is capable of intuiting my origins. If she were to play me more, if she were to elicit the notes beyond the notes, perhaps the concert of my life would come together.

The four of them continue to argue for a while. They embark into one heated exchange after another where the flaws of each are paraded and stoned by all. Without alcohol, the stabs are shorter but forceful. They come to the verge of dissolution, they look into the precipice, and they pull themselves back to solid ground. And it becomes obvious to me that the only element that keeps these four individuals together is music. Music forms the web that keeps them from falling apart even if that music waters away between their fingers.

What are the chances they will succeed? What are the real possibilities they will play the new piece and satisfy Amédée or the critics, if any care to come and listen? Would The Argonauts create thunder and light up the dark cloud engulfing them? Even a more personal question, why do I entertain these concerns? Should I not simply sing my best and avoid getting entangled in this insalubrious nexus?

Without clear answers, all I can do is join the circus. I must go along with The Argonauts and support their decisions. If Darío wants to play me, I will reluctantly cooperate. If Kiara were to play me, I would reach Nirvana, but a quiet one—my own personal glory. If no hands were to play me at all, I would still hum a melody and show the world what I am capable of doing. But, does the world care? Does it matter to the universe if I sound as a prodigious instrument or as a screeching cat?

Leon leaves the room precipitously, and everyone sighs for they expect he will go to *El Raval* in search for dope. It will be a pity if he gets high just when he finally decides to confront Darío. Not that Darío cares much for what Leon has to say, but the fact that he criticizes him in front of Kiara and Angelo is inspiring. At least, inspiring to me. I have yet to see any real opposition from Kiara or Angelo. They simply go ahead with Darío's plans in spite of his idiocy. Every group needs a leader, even if flawed. And at this point, The Argonauts need Darío. But I know the universe does not need him the same.

The arguments die away in Leon's absence. They stop talking to each other, and an uncomfortable silence grows inside the room. Kiara stays next to me, and from time to time touches my body. Angelo picks up a magazine and pretends to be interested in the cover. He does not open the magazine to read any of the articles. Darío walks around the room, taking occasional peeks outside the window. I am tempted to hum loudly but hold back my impulses, for the moment is not conducive to dissent. There will be better moments to infringe damage if I so need. Darío goes to the kitchen and after a few minutes comes back to announce that he just made coffee. Nobody moves, nobody thanks him. He gets a cup for himself and pours a shot of whiskey into it.

—This is just what I need.

—It won't make a difference.

—You can do the same, Angelo.

—It won't make a difference.

—What should the difference be?

—There's no difference to be had.

—Brilliant! I like your enthusiasm.

In one swig, Darío empties the cup and prepares himself another one. This time the shot of whiskey seems much longer. He continues to walk around the room evading eye contact with Kiara or Angelo. He sits next to me, holding the cup of coffee in one hand and reaching for my body with the other. But before he gets to touch me, Kiara slaps his hand just like she did to the little devil yesterday. The unexpected aggression makes Darío jump to his feet and child away to the window where he seems to start crying. Kiara then touches my belly and caresses my ribs. Darío watches as she bestows her tenderness on me. He then wails loudly and spits out a mouthful of the coffee and whiskey mix. Embarrassed, Darío runs to the kitchen and fetches a rag to clean the floor and his shoes. And neither Kiara nor Angelo raise their eyes to regard the spectacle. But they do look up as the front door opens and Leon storms into the room with clear eyes and his cello in tow.

In the center of the room, Leon places a chair and sits on it, the body of his cello between his legs, his left hand ready to slide up and down the long fingerboard. He does not bring any sheet music with him. What he wants to play must be readily available somewhere in the vast lake of his somnambulant self. His face seems relaxed, impassive even, but not as the result of a dope hit. His gaze moves around the room, touching each of the other Argonauts in the center of their foreheads. No malice, no critical sly, just a gentle nudge. He takes a deep breath, taking in the entire world with it, and begins to play one long and conciliatory note. He then starts to weave a series of notes within the range of one octave. And the simple melody surrounds us all, isolating us from everything that exists outside of this moment and this space. This music builds a dome that encompasses all the feelings and fears, all the discourse and distaste, all the hope and heresy alive in this room. Inside this dome, The Argonauts breathe each other's breath.

—How do we sound? Does anybody know how we really sound?

—Does it matter?

—If it matters to you, it matters to me.

—Yes, but does it really matter?

—If it didn't matter, why would we be playing at all?

—Who says it doesn't matter?

—Nobody said just that.

—Our problem is that we have too many doubts.

—Who has doubts?

—Don't we all?

—Leon has no doubts. Listen to the way he's playing.

—Is he playing or is he thinking out loud?

—I doubt that he's playing anything.

—But why do you doubt that?

—I don't know. I just do.

—He's feeling something. There's no doubt about that.

—How about yourself, do you play or do you feel?

—What's the difference?

—There's a difference. Sometimes I have intense feelings when I'm not playing anything.

—Wouldn't that be a waste of your talent?

—Perhaps. Do you feel something right now?

—Yes, of course, I do.

—Why not pick up your violin and play what you feel?

—I don't have my violin with me.

—Then play the violin you keep on touching.

Protected by the universal benevolence inside the dome, Kiara elevates my body and starts playing and feeling, a thin melodic line. The feeling floats in the air and gives itself to all. I cannot discern exactly what this feeling is, even when it comes through my own voice. A sense of warmth, perhaps… A sense of yearning, an oceanic sense. The melody turns and twists before layering itself softly over the basso continuo that Leon continues to play in the background. And together, both melodic lines glide as if one.

Kiara hands me over to Angelo who accepts me like a child getting a new toy. Without much effort, he starts to play a little allegretto, and the joyful feeling infuses the air inside the dome. The mischievous melodic line plays tricks with the basso continuo, hiding under it, jumping up and down, running ahead of it and stopping—the exuberant energy rattles inside my body. But with the same ease, as he accepted me, he turns me over to Darío. The abrupt change of hands takes me by surprise and makes my body contract at once. Time stops. Does time stop or does my joy come to a full stop? Easy, easy... I must relax my body. In the spirit of reconciliation, I take on Darío's chin and hands as if I have never known them before. He digs in with the Mongol hair.

Leon continues to play, but the absorbency of his melodic line begins to falter. The dome threatens to cave in and leave The Argonauts exposed, once more, to the raw dysfunctionality of their interactions. Darío does his best to modulate his playing. He treats me with renewed tenderness as if he were playing me for the first time. I keep my voice within the known register and eliminate any unintended sound. Leon then enters into a repetitive structure that permits him to oscillate over time without tearing or puncturing the dome. He seems to favor this move and renews his bowing intensity to support the integrity of the dome. This time, time counts. The other Argonauts hold their breath and hope for a peaceful resolution to this unstaged and awkward trial. Darío needs to show that he can play me without destroying the delicate balance of the dome. They all know this impromptu rehearsal is more real than the previous ones. At least I am not the one on trial, Darío is.

The beauty of playing oscillating structures is that one's mind is free to travel and explore. As I glide over pulsating strings that reappear slightly shifting with each recurrence, I consider the unresolved dilemmas embedded inside each of The Argonauts. I wonder if Angelo ever wanted to play the violin instead of the viola. I also wonder if he knows he is beautiful. Maybe beauty is enough for him. Why bother playing his best if he is already beautiful? And Leon. He plays his best, but that is not enough for him. He needs that other reality. The one where everything is altered yielding a more intense reality than the original one. I wonder which version is more real to him. And Darío. Buried under his own weight, his own self. Looking for ways to remain relevant. Would he ever stop being himself so that he finally gets the chance to be who he is? And Kiara. My eternal Kiara. Would she ever…

Tribulations do not procreate under the dome. Only a green truce takes root under its cover. And for as long as the cello and I keep accumulating one layer of harmony over another, The Argonauts manage to breathe a facile air. Without making much noise, Angelo heads for the door of the flat and whooshes himself away. Then I watch as Kiara takes leave after him, her hands flowing and not touching me. I sense the vacuum in the room, but Leon and Darío seem to ignore the two absences. Leon then begins to diminish the pressure of his bowing, bringing the volume of the cello to a bare whisper. The dome does not collapse to the ground; it simply lands softly. And with the same solemnity with which he walked into the flat earlier, he leaves with his cello and his dignity.

All alone, Darío maintains his composure. He does not let the music die. I feel even pressure on my strings, allowing me to sustain my voice undamaged. He then makes the harmonic layers disappear one by one closing with a diminuendo. I take a deep breath.

In the naked absence of the other Argonauts, Darío waits for the air to come to a still stance, and once he feels in supreme control of his domain, he grabs me and bursts outside the door of his flat. He climbs the narrow stairwell all the way up to a door that guards the roof terrace. He tries to open that door, but it does not want to open. He leans against it and pushes with his shoulder, but the door does not open. He then takes a step back and kicks the door hard, he kicks it hard, and the door opens up, and the mountains of the moon are waiting. Darío steps out on the roof and realizes there is only a small space for him to stand. He is careful to place his feet firmly at the edge of the roof. And with all his might, he swings my body around, lifting me into the upper layers of a night dark.

The moon shines a shameless light, drunk, spilling everything. I take the blubbering of the moon on my skin as I take life unexpected. I simply love the feel of nature bland, unaltered. And when Darío forms a bond with the essence of the moonlight, I know he is at the verge of playing real music. But what is real music for Darío? I have yet to know. Better not to infer what music is supposed to be, for the likelihood of reaching an answer is rather poor. I should just enjoy the moment dark and listen to the bells strike midnight. At the top of the night, after the twelve strikes, Darío settles me down. He dreams of a night with a moon like this one and with bells to impregnate the still air. But he also dreams of a night with my voice and the flesh of Kiara, one and the same, traversing his body. Darío is a simple animal: carnal joy, a limited sense of identity, a yearning for eternity. What else is there for him?

In the center of his dreams, not the center of my reality, Darío aspires to a grand status in the world of music. His entire discourse is one of advancement and positioning in the field of chamber music. A travesty of sorts, for chamber music is nothing other than the history of multiple relationships among four inadequate people. Real music played in a small chamber, in the presence of admirers of instruments and players, is a myth in this world. But we all need myths to make sense of our existence. And when Darío comes out to engage with the night in real terms, he is acknowledging that the night has a revealing power and that he better listen to it.

And in the beginning, the sounds of the invertebrate take over the night. What else could be expected from people who intend on making their mark when nobody else is listening or paying attention? Then come the sounds of dogs barking or a choir singing. Then comes the sound of a small orchestra trying to make their mark. Then comes the sound of a solo violin. And for a moment, I need to concentrate and figure out if I am the instrument singing or if another violin is to blame. But as I settle and listen to the music under the cloak of the moon, my voice, or a voice that imitates mine, seems to sound sounds.

But if I were to have a voice to call my own, would it not be the same voice whether Darío or Kiara play me? Or even more, would not that voice be available to me to hum or to use inside my case when no hands touch my strings? I would think so; but somehow, I continue to entangle my voice with the sonic effect of the hands that play me. Am I an autonomous instrument or a played wooden box? But what I believe I am, may be of no consequence if the true nature of myself is to exist as a servile instrument. And if that were the case, I rather live in the hands of Kiara than in the hands of a person like Darío. This, a situation I do not decide. I may influence their moods with my contortionist moves, but the plain truth is that I am a dependent box.

Darío becomes restless under the judging light of the moon. He starts to shift his weight from one foot to the other. And before the bells strike one, he abandons the roof and heads all the way down to the first floor of the building dragging me along. He then steps outside into the narrow street and decides to traverse the *Ciutat Vella* in search of Amédée. After meandering for a while, he reaches the end of a street that promises nothing. There is the gate of a building and a plate with names of people who live or may have lived in this place. He looks at the plate for a minute and finds no clear indication that Amédée either lives here now or has ever lived here before. Nevertheless, Darío rings one of the flats and the voice of a man answers.

—*Sí, dígame.*

—*El señor Amédée?*

—*Sí.*

—*Soy Darío.*

—*Que sorpresa. En qué le puedo servir a esta hora?*

—*Necesito hablar con usted.*

—*Bueno, suba al primer piso. Segunda puerta a la derecha.*

Darío presses me hard against his body and takes the few steps up the stairs to the first floor. In the dim light, he looks for a door with the name of "Amédée" printed on it. The doors have no names on them, so he follows the directions from the man who answered and knocks on the second door to the right. No response. He knocks again a little bit harder this time. Nobody answers. He then stands still, looking at the door, I guess hoping that someone will open up and ask him inside. But nobody opens the door. Darío walks downstairs to the ground floor and the gate of the building. He rings the same apartment again. This time there is only silence.

*****

The sound of someone knocking at the door fills the room with unmistakable tenderness. And when Darío opens the door, my impressions are confirmed at once. Only Kiara's knuckles can impart such warmth. They greet each other as if nothing happened yesterday. The fact that they argued does not register in the tone of their voices or the balance of their gestures.

Darío, sober at this time of the morning, tries to get close to Kiara and kiss her shoulder. The attempt fails for Kiara turns away from him and, without saying a word, stares at him with impassive eyes. The way it should be. The way it should always be. And if I could shriek at the highest pitch of my E string, I would. But the danger ends at once when Kiara starts to talk.

—Amédée is desperately looking for you.

—I was looking for him last night.

—Did you get to speak with him?

—No... He was in his flat but then he wasn't.

—Do you know where he lives?

—I'm not sure.

—Well, he says there'll be a change of venues.

—A change of venues at this time? What's he proposing?

—He wouldn't tell me. He said he wants to speak with you first.

—Yes, I went looking for him last night.

—Did you know something about this already?

—No, I wasn't aware of any changes.

—So why did you go looking for him?

—I'm not sure.

A silence rains inside the room, wetting every surface and casting doubts. A silence infiltrating the space between thought and action. Completely doused by this silence, Kiara leaves Darío behind and comes in the direction where I rest inside my case, my cover open, everything open. As she starts to reach for my body, Darío comes behind her and once again tries to kiss her shoulders and her neck. No… no, never again. I cannot let this happen. I need to stop this at once. So I contract every one of my wooden fibers, the maple of my back and ribs, the spruce of my belly. I stretch my ebony neck and pull with all the force I can muster. I let all the air out of my f-holes and contract more and more. My neural cords, stretched to the maximum, dig hard into my bridge, and I feel them cutting me. I take a deep breath, and with Apollonian might, I tighten everything, everything until my E string bursts sending a sharp pain through my body and whipping the air like a serpent's tongue. And at the snapping of the string, Kiara pushes Darío away from her and spits on his face. She is the serpent now.

—Don't touch me.

—You didn't have to…

—I said, don't touch me.

—What is it with you?

—I don't want your hands on me.

—Then why did you come to see me?

—I didn't come here to see you. I came to tell you something.

—Well, you already told me. Now what?

—Nothing, Darío. Nothing.

She picks me up with both hands and examines the damage. She unwinds half of my E string from the tuning peg and dislodges the other half from the tailpiece. I feel a certain imbalance in the forces that keep my body straight as if my left side was looser and my right side tighter. I am afraid I may twist over to my right side. To prevent any such twist, I tense the wooden fibers on my left and hope for a new string soon. While Kiara is busy nursing me, Darío comes close to her once more. But this time he does not try to touch or kiss her. He only observes what she is doing and then commands her.

—I think you should leave now.

—Who will take care of the violin?

—I will. I'll put a new string right away. But I want you to leave at once.

—Are you afraid of me?

—I'm not afraid of you. I'm afraid of myself.

—Your destructive self?

—Leave now, I say.

—Darío, what do you really want?

—What's the point in wanting? Nothing ever comes through.

—I don't see it that way.

—That's because you don't see.

—I'll leave now. Isn't that what you want?

—That's what needs to happen.

Kiara lays me down inside my case. The inner contours of the case trap my body in a green, velvety way. The fitted form will help me keep my natural form, at least until Darío decides to give me a new string. And from my supine position, I hear Kiara's steps moving toward the door, and I hear the door closing behind her. They do not say anything to each other. Her departure is dry.

Inside the room, I feel a wanting floating in the air. Darío wanting to hold Kiara comprises a large portion of that air mass. And Darío also wanting to play unique music, wanting to emerge from the gloom that surrounds him. And also, his wanting to dominate my body, to force me into playing like a virtuoso from Cremona. And Amédée wanting to find Darío to tell him about something he wants. Then, there is Kiara wanting to abandon her violin and play me instead. This wanting could be a figment of my imagination, or perhaps my own wanting projected onto her. She seems to want to hold me; I think she does. I want her to want that. I so desire.

Nothing indicates that Darío is about to fit me with the string I need. He sits spreading his legs apart, bent forward, his head hanging between his legs, his arms held up by his knees, the very spectacle of a desecrated man. I wonder if he is sorry for his treatment of Kiara, for his rapacious behavior. Or maybe he is not critical of himself, only angry that he failed to conquer her. I fear sharing the room with him under this leaden solitude. And all I hope is for time to speed up its tempo, to deliver me to another moment away from this one. But hoping does nothing other than to accentuate this prostrating stasis.

After minutes or hours, I cannot tell, I hear Darío blow air through his nose. I think I hear him think. He stands up, the mountain of himself growing from his previous flatness as he advances to where I am lying. He stops in front of my case and takes a long, languid look at me. What he sees in me, I do not really know. What he ultimately wants from me I do not know either. Maybe his disenchantment is not different from mine. Maybe we are both chasing that which we cannot grab.

Darío walks away into the shadows of his room and returns promptly with a shiny coil of Peter Infeld platinum E. He sits next to my case and takes me into his hands. With slow and deliberate movements, he begins the process of installing my new string. He is reconstructing my neural cords, healing the very damage I inflicted on myself. And in so doing, he is adding to my body. This external element, this metal string, will soon be an integral part of who I am. It will constitute a significant range of my voice with the capacity to take me to the highest pitch I can possibly reach. And once the transubstantiation is complete, he proceeds to stretch the string and bring it to its perfect and natural tone. Now I can relax my wooden fibers and breathe naturally.

Without much forethought, Darío grabs me and heads out into the streets of *Ciutat Vella* where the crowds are delirious and intoxicated with life. He retraces his steps and heads for the same street that left him without answers last night. Looking carefully at every gate for the name "Amédée," he finally reaches the one with the many nameplates, none of which he recognizes. This time he does not ring any bell, he waits until someone opens the gate, slips inside the building, climbs one flight of stairs, and comes to stand in front of the second door on his right just as he did last night. When he is about to knock, he stops his hand before it crashes against the wood of the door. Instead of knocking, he opens my case and pulls me out. Bow in hand, he starts to caress my strings inducing me to sing a penetrating melody I have never heard before. Contemporary, the melody, but from an unknown composer. Or at least unknown to me. And the melody seems to embody a cry for something, a moaning, perhaps a call for mercy. He makes me repeat the passage at a slower tempo, and this time the cry takes on a much deeper sense. It feels universal, like everyman's lament.

The response to my voice comes in the form of the door opening and light spilling into the hallway. The man who opens the door is Amédée. He first says nothing and allows for Darío to play the melody one more time. I modulate my voice to sound as splendid as I can, for I know I am being heard attentively. I resonate on my G string in a sublime fashion bestowing the melody with a depth as deep as Darío's disenchantment. This time I embody his thoughts. This time I allow him to speak through me.

Amédée takes Darío by the elbow, and without interrupting his playing, leads him inside the flat and positions him in the center of the salon where he is certain to listen to every note of the musical plight. I sustain my voice in its purest form, and every melodic inflection is the direct incarnation of Darío's thoughts and emotions. I take a step back from asserting myself as the violin that I am. This moment I become an instrument, instrumental in permitting the life of the other traverse through me.

When Darío finishes playing me, I make certain not to vibrate any longer. I mute my natural inner hum and let the silence between the two men speak for itself. They gaze at each other, perplexed, it seems, to be in each other's presence without any premonition that they would find themselves this way.

—How did you find me?

—I came looking for you.

—But why?

—That's what I'm not so sure about. I felt as if I needed to reveal something about The Argonauts.

—Did Kiara tell you I actually wanted to speak with you?

—She did this morning, but I had already found you last night.

—What do you mean?

—I came here last night.

—Darío, I wasn't here last night. I was in Sitges.

—That may be the case, but I spoke with you. Or maybe I didn't.

—Well, what is it that you want to tell me about The Argonauts?

—It may not be about the ensemble. It's more about myself.

—Isn't everything always personal, like the melody you were just playing?

—So, you know what I want to say. Don't you?

—I do.

Amédée stretches his arms in front of him, palms up, as if willing to support the weight of the world. Darío deposits my body on those stretched arms. I feel the snapping of a cord, umbilical this time, and once again, I return to my autonomous condition of an instrument of music. The last composer to hold me as a respectable instrument was Giambattista, and the results were extraordinary. This time I hope the proximity to the creative source will clarify my role in this conflicted world of The Argonauts.

A musical composition has two poles, which I might call the artistic and the esthetic: the artistic refers to the score created by the composer, and the esthetic to the realization accomplished by the performer. From this polarity, it follows that the aural experience of the musical composition cannot be completely identical with the score, or with the performance of the score, but half-way between the two. And that is how my body functions as an instrument, bridging the two poles. But I need more than that. I have urges, some of which are material, perhaps verging into carnal, but some undoubtedly sublime. To accept my condition as a mere bridge would consolidate my self as a lesser being.

—Darío, we have a wonderful opportunity. The Emerson Quartet cancelled their appearance at *L'Auditori*. We're invited to take their spot in the program.

—For the debut of your piece?

—Yes, next week.

—And the *Palau*? Would they release us?

—They're fine with the idea.

—That's fantastic!

—Yes, this is very good for all.

—Can we rehearse there?

—They'll grant us access. Once or twice.

—Why didn't you tell Kiara?

—Well, there're other details.

—What details?

—This very violin.

—What about this violin?

—You know, I wrote the piece for this violin.

—We all know that.

—Yes, but I've yet to hear the piece in its full splendor, the way I envisioned it.

—We still have another week to polish it, don't we?

—Darío, I don't know where this violin came from, but it sounds like no other.

—I agree, sometimes it does.

—But not in your hands.

—What are you trying to say?

—I'm not trying; I'm saying that we cannot take the risk…

—What are you really trying to say?

—I don't hear my music coming to its full potential in your hands.

Amédée takes a few steps back and turns away from Darío while still holding me in his arms. He lays me down on a red divan in the far corner of the salon and returns to face Darío.

—Amédée, what do you think you're doing?

—I want the violin to sound at its best.

—So do I. Can I please have my violin?

—This is a unique opportunity, Darío.

—Yes, this is a unique opportunity. We all need this kind of opportunity.

—Would you consider…

—There's nothing to consider. Can I have my violin?

—Does this violin really belong to you?

—This is nonsense!

The body of the man that plays me moves fast past the body of the man that dreams of me as the violin I know I am. And fiercely, Darío retrieves me from the redness of the divan. And without saying any other words, he erupts out of the flat leaving behind the place he found by chance, or by instinct, and sinks deep into the crowded street.

*****

Nothing can be more frightening than hearing the voice of a former abusive partner. Every abused being harbors those ominous sounds in his or her brain. And my body shakes, possibly at the same frequency as Madeleine's hands shake, when Maria's voice repeats over and over that this is the right block, that the enclosed garden is part of the university and that the street is called Granados. From the outdoor terrace where Darío is sitting and drinking his fourth glass of cava, Maria's voice can be heard. Clearly, French-accented, and

188

full of impudence. The two women recognize Darío from far away and wave at him. Their approach is imminent, and so is my misery. Their presence is only a confirmation that nothing is ever bad enough. They clearly know where they are heading, so this is not a coincidental encounter. Darío must need them here, or maybe he only needs Madeleine. But what is the prey to do without its predator? After numerous empty kisses, the two women sit next to Darío and ask the waiter for their respective glasses of cava. Madeleine looks at me as I lie here, immobile, and I cannot tell if she is content to see me again. Maria ignores me. I mean nothing to her.

They talk frivolities for a while, moving from the irrelevant to the immaterial. At one point they mention the rest of The Argonauts, but only in passing. Maria makes sure to stamp her opinion on every topic, and Madeleine rushes to agree with her. I am practically forgotten during this part of the conversation. A pathetic move for I suspect I am the reason for their visit to Barcelona. A few glasses of cava later, Madeleine gets closer to me and picks me up from my case. Her tenderness is not her own, for she is only free to care for anything when her puppeteer permits her. But while Madeleine becomes engrossed with me, Maria carries on a conversation with Darío that is certain to result in someone being hurt.

—More people will hear you at *L'Auditori*. People that count that is.

—Yes, but we're far from ready.

—That's what you told me. What's holding you back?

—I cannot rehearse the piece with that violin. I cannot make it sound right.

—That happened to me as well, remember?

—Yes, I do. But I know it has the capacity to produce magnificent sound, but not when it matters.

—Is it an issue of relevance?

—I think it is. I play with the same technique every time but I get different results.

—Are you saying this violin has a will of its own?

—No, I'm saying that it sounds different, worse, I should say when it matters most.

—So, what do you propose? Why did you ask me to come here?

—I want you to take the violin and rehearse the piece by yourself, away from The Argonauts and the concert hall. I'll pay you for this.

—What's the purpose?

—I'll get my confidence back, and maybe the violin will get used to sounding well.

—Why don't you swap violins with Kiara?

—Trust me, Madeleine; there're certain things I cannot do.

I have been traded before. I have been sold. But I have never been dismissed for disciplinary reasons. Yes, he may need to regain his confidence. But the fact that such confidence wavers is only a reflection of his wavering self, more precisely, an indication that his unkindness is boiling over. I doubt he wants The Argonauts to succeed or to celebrate Amédée's composition. What drives him is a fraught need to appear as a virtuous player in front of Kiara. As if her acceptance would make him what he is not.

As the afternoon comes down to a whisper, the prospect of Madeleine and Maria taking me with them becomes imminent. At this point, the three of them are subsumed under an alcoholic frenzy where absurdity turns into logic, and everyone loves each other too much. And since Madeleine never rejected the outrageous proposition, my near future is sealed. Darío pays the entire bill, and when they part ways, I find myself inside the case, hanging from Madeleine's shoulder, on the way to some corner of the world where I fear abuse will find me.

*****

On a narrow street, not far from Granados and the university, Maria insists on entering a lounge where the only people frolicking are women. Madeleine tries to keep on walking down the street, but Maria grabs the strap of my case and pulls Madeleine by the neck. We all end up inside the lounge and Maria finds a tight spot by the bar where the waitress is already asking what do they want to drink. Maria speaks loudly for both them and requests a bottle of cava. As the bubbles and the alcohol continue to enter their bodies, their gestures and words become increasingly brusque. Women come and go dressed in all sorts of attire. The colors are also maddening. But the worst of all is the music. I have heard troubled compositions, but nothing as exquisitely inhuman as the musical distortion that irks out from every corner of the bar and bounces from wall-to-wall and from head-to-head. A tall woman with a short dress approaches Madeleine and asks what is hanging from her shoulder. Maria interrupts the conversation and responds that nothing is hanging from any shoulder after which she proceeds to take my case and shove it between her legs. And when Madeleine tries to snatch my case again, Maria slaps her hands and gives her the most sinister look. This, the crudest omen of what is to come.

The bottle of cava runs dry. But the dull fact does not change Maria's enthusiasm who orders yet another bottle, and forces Madeleine to have the first glass. She tells her that alcohol is good for her, that she will feel less if she is drunk. Madeleine tries to swallow some of the cava, but she starts gagging and starts throwing up most of it. Maria steps back and wipes the liquid off of her hands and face. She then grabs Madeleine by the collar of her white shirt and squeezes really tight.

—You got your bile all over me.

—I don't, I mean, I'm sorry…

—You filthy bitch, you got me dirty.

—I didn't mean to.

—When I say swallow, you swallow.

—I will swallow.

—No, no, no… You swallow when I tell you.

With her free hand, Maria rams the bottle into Madeleine's mouth who tries to swallow but chokes on the wine and starts coughing and foaming out of her mouth. Maria lets go of the collar and Madeleine bends over and empties most of her stomach on the floor of the bar. People step aside, more concerned about getting dirty than about Madeleine's well-being. A young woman even starts clapping. When the rhythmic contractions of her stomach come to an end, Madeleine gets up, grabs my case, and runs out of the bar and into the fresh air of the street. She aims to run further down the street, but she staggers. She stumbles over the curb and comes down hard over my case. I find myself trapped between the harshness of the sidewalk below me and the limp body of

Madeleine above. I feel the pressure, but nothing seems to have broken. At least, nothing I can tell at this moment.

In a few seconds, Maria surges out of the bar in search of Madeleine. She quickly finds us and comes close to where we lie. She stands there and laughs, a hyena laugh, without offering to help Madeleine get on her feet. She keeps on laughing, and the sound makes me remember the old days when people without buboes laughed at the sight of disfigured legs, bloated and oozing, just to find themselves with buboes all over themselves a few days later. But that sort of poetic justice is not universal, and the likelihood that Maria will ever pay for her inflictions is minimal.

She goes back into the bar and returns with whatever is left of the bottle of cava. She sits next to us and pours herself a full glass. Between prolonged sips, she caresses Madeleine's hair. And with the edge of her skirt, she wipes the vomit from Madeleine's face. Her pianist hands are skillful, soft even.

—Madeleine, my Madeleine… Why do you do these things? Running away… Let me make it better for you. Here, here… My Madeleine… You will play this violin; you will play it well. I know you like how it sounds. Don't you? I like it too. Here, here… My Madeleine… I know you like to play it. But don't like it too much. My Madeleine…

THE DEAD

Today I find relief in being played by Madeleine. With much less tension and no need to excel, she allows me to sing unencumbered. This practice session becomes a dialogue; she gives me her tenderness, and I sing as she wishes. The lonesome green parrot is our witness. But this peaceful arrangement is shattered when Maria opens the door and walks into the room. Madeleine immediately tenses her body, and her arms lose the previous fluidity and grace. She digs harder than necessary with the Mongol hair and plays a few notes completely out of tune. The air becomes dense, and the music has no chance to grow open and alluring.

Maria sits by the piano and tries to accompany a simple passage of Beethoven's Violin Romance No. 2. She plays her part fairly well, but Madeleine's tempo is wrong, and she even misses one or two notes. They go on like this for a few bars until Maria closes the fallboard. And instead of appearing frustrated, Maria wears a placid smile on her face.

—That doesn't sound right. You're completely off.

—I can't help it. This thing is deviant.

—Isn't that what Darío said?

—Maybe that's what he implied.

—Why bother with it? Just give it back to him.

—I will. I certainly will.

But the moment Maria walks out of the room and her steps begin to die away behind the closed door, Madeline picks me up and becomes one with Beethoven's Romance No. 2. The sweet, innocent melody fills the room and drowns Maria's steps. The delicate youthful phrasing helps Madeleine find a brief respite. In her playing, all angst is now absent, suggesting that all is well. But as she knows all too clearly, this is far from the case.

Left alone, the rest of the day goes by, and the only memorable event is the intermittent singing of the parrot inside a white lattice cage. Once the room becomes quiet, the bird starts singing at uneven intervals producing remarkable sounds that mimic a variety of instruments. For a moment it sounds like a first-class violin and I can identify some of the nuances of Madeleine's playing. And with phenomenal ease, it changes its sound and turns into a well-tempered piano. It must be mimicking Maria. After singing a few melodies, the bird becomes eerily silent. Maybe it is eating, or poking under its feathers. Or maybe the bird is gathering its strength to sound like a full orchestra. But without any clear prompt, the bird begins to emit sounds again. This time I identify what seems like one or two voices murmuring in the distance. Yes, these are voices, but they are unintelligible to me. These voices go on for a while, talking to each other until the bird transforms them into the most harrowing of sounds. Not the sound of words anymore, but that of a disturbing moan. A long, low sound like that of a person expressing physical or mental suffering, or perhaps sexual pleasure. I am not sure which. The sounds are so real that I start wondering if perhaps this moaning is coming from the other side of the walls.

But just as abruptly as the parrot started to sing, it comes to a complete stop again. I remain alert waiting to hear more instruments or voices, but the bird seems to have run out of things to say. I can hear it moving inside the cage, shuffling, eating seeds, but there is no more singing. By this time, the natural light inside the room has started to wither away. And a loud silence penetrates my f-holes.

The room becomes a monumental absence. Absence of music, absence of moaning, absence of suffering, absence of a personal history, absence of a reason to be present. In this limbo, I hover uninterrupted by my bird comrade. I imagine the bliss of unawareness, the not knowing what we miss. Perhaps existing without the awareness of an absence is the most sublime experience of presence. If so, what do we need music for? Even when music does not involve any other senses, it is certain to arouse an aural experience, and therefore, a presence. If music then conjures a presence, would it not negate the possibility of this beautiful unawareness of absence? And if that were the case, the primordial purpose for my existence, the fundamental function of my violin nature, would deprive me and those around me access to the bliss of unawareness. But I should not be dammed for what I am.

The absence, frail and unsustainable, implodes when the sound of a moaning voice invades the room once more—this time more intense and wretched than before. It cannot be the parrot singing because the sound clearly comes from the other side of the door. It filters into the room through a sliver at the bottom of the door, which also allows light to come in. The moaning grows and grows. For a moment it sounds more distant, but then it comes as a cresting wave closer to the door. Then a crash, a thunder. A heavy mass pools at the bottom of the door blocking the filtering light. The moaning stops completely, and all I hear is the incessant breathing of a person on the other side of the door, a flow of air moving in and out, a suffocating agony, maybe a whimper.

The person stands up from the floor and pushes the door open. Light rushes into the room ahead of a naked body which trails behind. Once I manage to get a glimpse, I recognize the face of Madeleine approaching me. Nothing different on her face, just a dejected and empty expression. But when she reaches to hold me, I notice how her fingers seem transformed. The thumb on her left hand is twice its normal size and blue at the base. And the index finger is bent in the most unnatural way. This is no accident; this is the result of abuse. She tries to hold me with her left hand, but my fingerboard barely fits between those two massacred fingers. She then tries to hold me up with her open palm, but her other fingers do not reach my neural cords. She cannot play me like this. And that may be better for I fear more abuse will come if Maria hears my voice. Yes, Maria, who else would treat her this way?

And just as I am trying to imagine what could have really happened, a silhouette grows at the door, blocking the light. The faceless form stands in silence, watching what Madeleine and I are doing. Madeleine's maimed hand starts shaking, and she lays me down next to her. She gathers herself, stands straight, and looks at the silhouette which remains moored to the door. I hear the incessant breathing again coming from Madeleine's lungs; a staccato rhythm that starts to accelerate its tempo until it gets interrupted by the austere words coming from the silhouette.

—Here's the scarf.

—I can't do it.

—Do it to me.

—No, Maria. I don't want to.

—You do what I tell you.

In full nakedness, Maria enters the room and comes to kneel in front of Madeleine but facing away from her. She carries a red silk scarf tightly strung between her hands. She turns around and upwards and tries to make eye contact with Madeleine.

—Look at me, not at that useless piece of wood.

—I don't want to do this again.

—If you don't hurt me, I will hurt you more.

Maria wraps the scarf around her neck and gives the two loose ends to Madeleine.

—Now, pull hard.

—No, Maria. My hand hurts.

—You better do it.

Madeleine starts to pull from both ends of the scarf. She loosens the tension for a moment to adjust the scarf around the good fingers on her left hand. She continues to exert force. Maria starts to rock back and forth on her knees, *andante ma non troppo.*

—Pull harder, you bitch.

—My hand hurts.

—Pull, pull!

Madeleine continues to stretch the ends of the scarf as hard as she can. And the harder she pulls, the slower Maria rocks on her knees. Maria stops rocking at once and with her right hand, starts to touch herself between her legs in the most frenetic way. She then starts to gasp, and her eyes roll back inside their sockets. Above the scarf, her neck and face turn purple, especially her lips and tongue out of which a few words try to come out, but all I hear is a shallow gasp. She then collapses on the floor. The color purple then covers her from the neck up, like a hood.

THE OBJECT OF DESIRE

Instead of confidence, a story of death is what Madeleine delivers when she deposits my body into Darío's arms. He cannot relate to the wrenching experience Madeleine went through. All he does is to look at me in a stupor. He pays Madeleine what he had promised and does not ask a single question about what happened. The size of someone else's misery is always measured against that of our own. A relative world this is. And as such, Darío succumbs to the most elemental self-centered doom.

The next few days will test my capacity to exist. I could exist as a mere instrument and sing on demand. I could exist as a superb instrument and sing beyond expectations. I could also sabotage the concert and bring myself and everyone else down with me. I could, like Darío, try to bring Kiara closer to me. There are many things I can do, but what escapes me, what has proven an impossible feat, is to select the hands that play me. I have and will continue to master my voice, but I have yet to master my master. And hell has taunted me for that very reason. From being forsaken in damp rooms, to receiving blows of anger, to being cheaply traded and sold, to being operated on by atrocious luthiers. All of this because my will is subordinate to the will of others.

I wait in anticipation for the afternoon and a possible trip to *L'Auditori.* Kiara must be wondering what happened to me. Or maybe not. Maybe the rest of The Argonauts have forgotten me. And as I ponder these and other irreverent ideas, Darío walks back and forth in the flat, making sure not to come close to me. He circles around, avoiding me all day. This makes me feel as if I was contagious as if my body was covered by oozing buboes.

In this abysmal absence of music, certitude, or tenderness, I resort to the one practice that can bring me solace. I hum. I hum lovingly. I conjure the tiny vibrations inherent to every one of my spruce and maple fibers—that capacity to sway as prime matter deep in the forest, untouched by man. And the notes I emit create a personal harmony that grows out of past seasons and loose winds. And I know that no matter what happens with The Argonauts, or whose hands play me, this is my own private concert, the music I play to myself as a violin.

Today plays itself out, and the late hours replace the early hours just to be replaced in turn by tomorrow's early hours again. A day enters, and I receive it. Darío makes no gesture to indicate what the immediate destiny of the day will be. I want to imagine that The Argonauts will rehearse and that I will have a chance to sing. I want to imagine Kiara wants to hear my voice today. I really want to imagine that Kiara wants to touch me. No, even further, I am certain that Kiara needs to touch me. But the truth is that I can imagine whatever I want or project my needs onto others. To no avail, for reality is clearly not what we want, and barely what we need.

Today, at four in the afternoon, as per the lazy clock, Darío tucks me into my case and springs out of the flat with such determination that I wonder if he is itching somewhere. He walks fast, past a slower crowd of Chinese tourists, and dives into the mouth of the metro. My memories of the underground force me to keep my guard up and to distrust anyone getting close to me. Nothing good ever breeds in this nefarious place. And the image of swimming rodents drags me into the faint memory of the black lagoon and the bodies of the three Venetians. I suspect I will soon be in the company of another three instruments. But nothing like the Venetians—gods and goddesses they were.

When we emerge in *Plaça de les Glòries* and start walking toward *L'Auditori*, I feel the excitement of Kiara's proximity and the dread of the failure to come. Even if Darío is not ultimately responsible for his own failure, even if I play a significant role in his demise, I still feel as if the failure is not my responsibility. We make our way into Hall #4, the one dedicated to Alicia de Larrocha, the little giant, and to my surprise, the rest of The Argonauts are already here practicing an impossible passage.

Nobody stops playing to greet Darío. After a while, they put the instruments down and engage in a discussion about the difficult piece they are trying to conquer. So Darío pulls up a chair and joins the circle. He brings me up to his shoulder and makes eye contact with the rest of them.

—What are we playing?

—Shostakovich.

—Why are we not playing Amédée?

—Because we only have two more days.

—Exactly.

—We're doomed, Darío.

—Who're you to say that?

—An honest junky, you may say.

—I never called you a "junky," Leon.

—It's not what you say, Darío.

—Enough. Amédée's first movement. *Da Capo al Fine.*

The Argonauts retain a modicum of loyalty in spite of their dysfunctional antics. Otherwise, they would not remain together. And drawing from that infirm strength, they bring their instruments together in a mediocre rendition of

Amédée's composition. This time I sing in my normal voice without any attempts on my part to alter the quality or flow of the playing. So, the lackluster performance is not my fault. Maybe Leon's, he is clearly upset, and his playing shows it very well. And Angelo seems bored. As for Kiara, she must be dreaming about something for her hands tremble like unquiet butterflies. Before moving on to a disastrous second movement, Darío draws everyone's attention.

—This is for real. The opportunity is real. We have to do well.

—Why don't you start by deciding what violin to play?

—I'm sticking with this one once and for all.

—Really? The bastard…

The rehearsal begins to sag under the weight of the shared disappointment. The problem is not with intonation or tempo, but with a sense of vacuity, almost palpable, flooding the performance. If music were to have a scent, this performance would be considered a pestilent one. Even after an extraordinary effort, we only manage to go over Amédée's composition once. At the end of the piece, without Darío having to say anything to this effect, The Argonauts put away their instruments and leave *L'Auditori* as defeated soldiers. In two days we will come together again, and a turn in my destiny is bound to happen. I feel it in my every fiber.

*****

If music is the answer to the mysteries of life, The Argonauts are bound to find some revelations in today's concert. Not because they will play better or worse than expected, but because of the impending confluence of opposing desires. Darío tightens his black bow tie once more. He regards himself in the mirror and tightens it yet again. Kiara tries to look at her own reflection, but there is no space for her in the mirror. Leon seems to be rehearsing the piece in his mind, his eyes closed, his fingers fingering the air while rocking back and forth at a low frequency. Nobody says a word to each other, and they avoid each other's gazes. The most pronounced detachment is that of Angelo, who sits facing the corner of the rehearsal room as if punished.

Outside the rehearsal room, the frantic steps of people walking up and down create a bluish noise on top of which I almost hear the nervous thoughts of The Argonauts. The sound engineer opens the door, and when confronted with the deep dejection in front of her, she closes the door and leaves at once. Leon now pulls a cigarette and attempts to light it with his nervous fingers. Before he manages to succeed, Darío snatches the cigarette from his hands, throws it on the floor, and crushes it with the tip of his black shoe. He does not respond, Leon, he continues his autonomous rehearsal, unaltered. I try to listen for the inner music of the other instruments but register nothing. I know that when the prelude to a piece of music is only silence, the piece itself is dead, or moribund at best. It has already started to die inside the minds of the musicians and their instruments, and as a result, it silences them. And I have no doubt that Amédée's composition is beginning to die a little inside The Argonaut's minds. But their communal angst is more pressing; it deals with unresolved yearnings and elemental uncertainties. And I wonder if Amédée's composition will be capable of delivering them from their silent prelude.

The inevitable moment comes when Amédée pokes his

head into the room and, in spite of the unwelcoming air, lets himself in. He may still hope The Argonauts will perform his composition brilliantly. But his facial expression betrays him. It reveals that if he could, he would kneel down and weep with all of us, Argonauts and instruments alike. Instead, he grabs a chair and sits down. And acknowledging the reigning silence in the room, he remains silent as well. The bluish noise sipping from the outside becomes louder and louder as the audience in *L'Auditori* seems ready for the start of the concert. After a handful of minutes during which nothing audible transpired inside the room, a knock on the door announces that we must take the stage.

Darío holds me tight and leads The Argonauts through the back door of the stage. The warm applause fails to eliminate the uneasy sense of marching into the gallows. If the audience knew how little The Argonauts were expecting of themselves, they would have applauded louder or run for the exit. But music is magical, and we are supposed to be musical wizards. The audience needs us to conjure an aural experience outside the realm of their expectations. Yes, this is an ordinary performance, but they demand a little levitating adventure. Then the lights are slightly lowered, and we take our respective positions forming a semi-circle. Darío takes the first chair on the left, followed by Kiara, Angelo, and finally Leon. Of all the naked hands on stage, the only ones that tremble are the ones holding me. And not only are Darío's hands unsteady, but sweat starts to drip from his forehead even before playing a single note.

The emcee proclaims The Argonauts as a leading quartet performing contemporary classical music, and adds that the audience should feel honored to listen to the world premiere of a piece by Amédée, and asserts that they will witness something unusual. This last assertion, our performance as something unusual, is precisely what I aim to provide. But as I sense the hesitation in Darío's trembling hands, I begin to doubt myself. Even if he were to press my fingerboard in the wrong spot, missing by half a note, I could correct the mistake and sing mostly in tune. But if his mistakes become crass and exorbitant, we will be certainly doomed. And with the slightest nod of his head, Darío throws The Argonauts into the deepest abyss they have ever fathomed.

Right from the start, on the first few bars, Darío presses hard with the Mongol hair to the point that my neural cords screech, a most disagreeable sound that certainly reaches the audience. His steely left thumb squeezes my neck, making him miss a couple of notes when moving from third to the first position. Then he plays only one string in some double stops. The audience will not tell the difference, but Amédée certainly will. Everyone else manages to play perfectly well. Kiara's hands move with supreme delicacy, and I only wished she was playing me. In reality, that is all I desire. But I am aware that life contains but two tragedies: the first one is not to get your heart's desire; the second one is actually to get it. My destiny, however, is a wicked one, and I am not its master. And in spite of Darío's caustic playing, the first movement needs to come to an end. And it does.

Disappointed, a few people in the audience make a calculated and surreptitious move and leave the concert hall between the first and second movements. Others look at their watches more than necessary—all ominous signs. But we launch into the second movement; nevertheless, an *adagietto fugato*, hoping for redemption. The slower tempo allows

Darío to focus on intonation and precise phrasing. This time the music glides with more ease. Nevertheless, sustaining longer notes proves difficult for Darío. The rest of The Argonauts try to cover for him by increasing the volume of sound coming from their instruments. They use as much hair as possible, play closer to the bridge, and increase the vibrato. But the second movement suffers, and so does the audience that shows signs of becoming increasingly uneasy.

The third movement proposes a faster tempo, *an allegro con bravura*. The Argonauts manage almost unharmed until the middle of the movement when Darío needs to hold a long note two octaves above the first G on my E string. To steady his trembling right hand, Darío presses hard on the bow. And as he reaches all the way with the frog of the bow, my E string bursts under the pressure and I scream in acute pain. His face goes from red to white, his position from sitting to standing, all in the fraction of a second. Darío excuses himself to the audience and leaves through the backdoor, dragging me along.

In the rehearsal room, he rummages through my case until he finds a replacement string. He is quick to untangle the dead filament still rolled around one of my pegs. I watch and sense his every move under the rain of sweat and fugitive tears. He tightens the string and fiddles with the fine tuner until I sing a clear open E. He then lays me on a chair and takes a step back. He stares at me for a few seconds, and all the waters of his face coalesce. I marvel at the transformation happening in front of me. His eyes soften, his lips form a horizontal line, and he loosens the clench of his jaw. With kindness unnatural to him, Darío picks me up and slowly makes his way back to the stage where the rest of The Argonauts and the audience await him. He seems to traverse through his mind. If all that we are is the result of what we have thought. If the mind is everything, really everything, then Darío is about to become that what he thinks. So instead of returning to his original position, Darío takes Kiara by her hands and leads her to the chair of the first violin. He exchanges the violins, taking the second violin away from her and depositing my body on her hands. And before sitting on the second chair, he declares *Da Capo al Fine*.

Kiara raises me up to her chin, a motion that is bound to alter my destiny. I understand that everything comes to us from others, and that to be is to belong to someone. In this very moment, the name whispered to me by the luthier in Nice returns to my mind: Hieronimo Venier. You who created me, why did you abandon me? Was my sound unworthy? Did the black death force your hand? Or was I just a lesser violin? But before I can find an answer to my questions, a sharp and short inhalation from Kiara signals the start of the third movement, *allegro con bravura*.

The Argonauts follow her with confidence. I know she yearns to play first violin. She desires it as much as I desire for her hands to play me. And her fingers lead my voice, and my voice penetrates the air, and we both fill the concert hall in perfect harmony. And her artistry becomes manifest as a veritable miracle. Then the music expands and enters into the minds of every listener, changing them, making them witnesses to the secret miracle. And every note transcends time as we advance, not through the score, but through our desires. With every fiber of my body I vibrate. With every breath I sing. And with every gesture Kiara flourishes. This continues until the seams that hold my wooden body unbind.

And my body parts begin to migrate, shifting my ancestral integrity. I burst outward and dematerialize in front of the perplexed audience. Fractured into multiple facets, I merge with the musical notes and the surrounding space—disembodied. And Kiara and I continue flourishing and yearning until we reach this moment when we touch that which we cannot possess.

JORGE ARMENTEROS was born in Cuba, his family leaving for Madrid, Spain, then Tampa, Florida, before finally settling in Puerto Rico. After graduating from Harvard University, he acquired an MD at the University of Puerto Rico and completed his residency in psychiatry at Bellevue Hospital in New York City, later obtaining an MA in Spanish and Latin American Literature at New York University and an MFA in Creative Writing at Lesley University. Armenteros is the author of the 2015 International Latino Book Award winner *The Book of I* (Jaded Ibis Press), and the *Striped Tunic Trilogy: Air*, *The Roar of the River*, and *The Spiral of Words* (Spuyten Duyvil Press). His author interviews and book reviews have appeared in The Writer's Chronicle, American Book Review, Rain Taxi, and Gargoyle. Armenteros resides in the South of France.

www.ingramcontent.com/pod-product-compliance
Lightning Source LLC
Chambersburg PA
CBHW011212190726
48288CB00013B/3416